FARM FEUD

Brian "Smitty" Smith

HARPER
alley

An Imprint of HarperCollinsPublishers

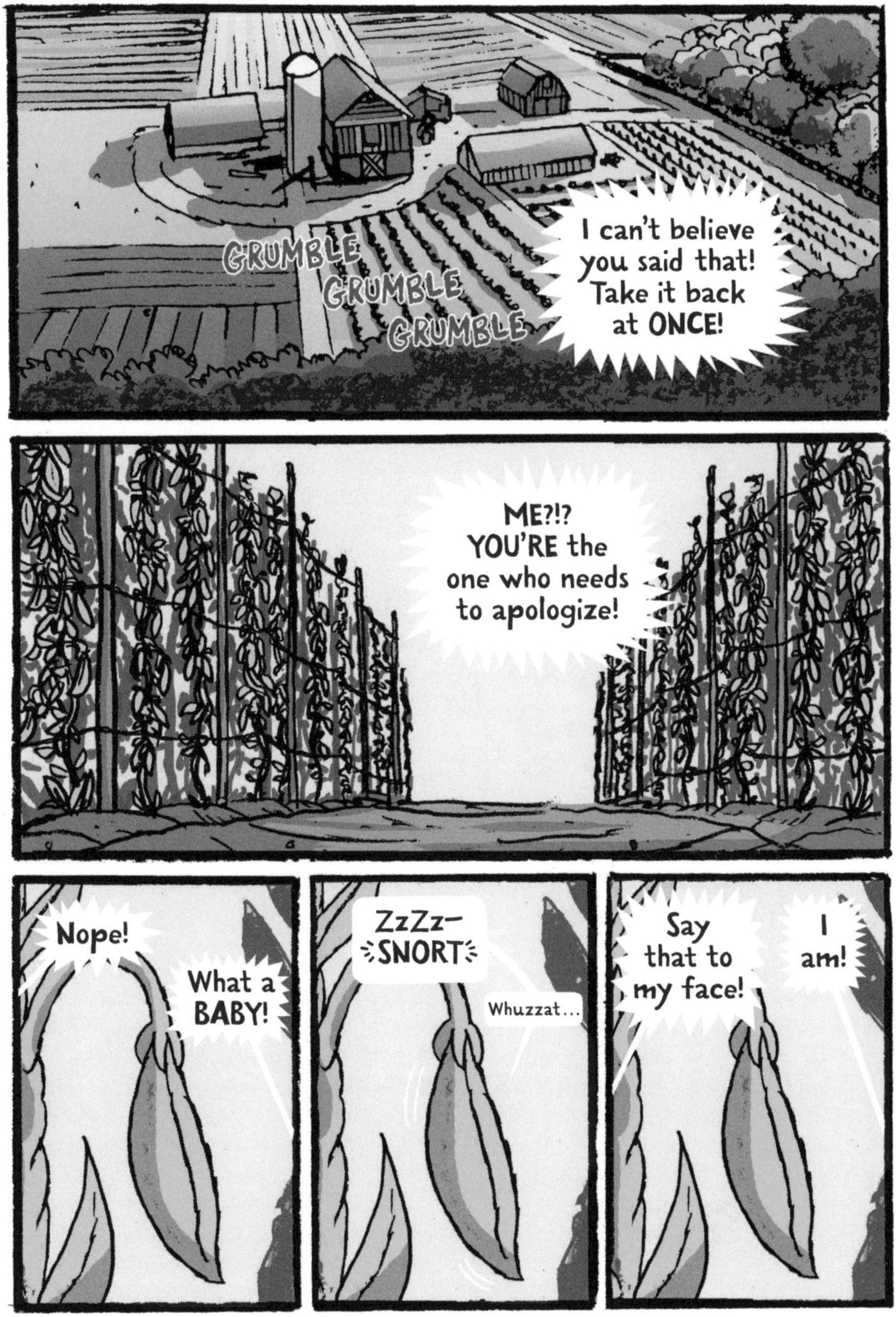
GRUMBLE
GRUMBLE
GRUMBLE
I can't believe you said that! Take it back at ONCE!
ME?!? YOU'RE the one who needs to apologize!
Nope!
What a BABY!
ZzZz-SNORT
Whuzzat...
Say that to my face!
I am!

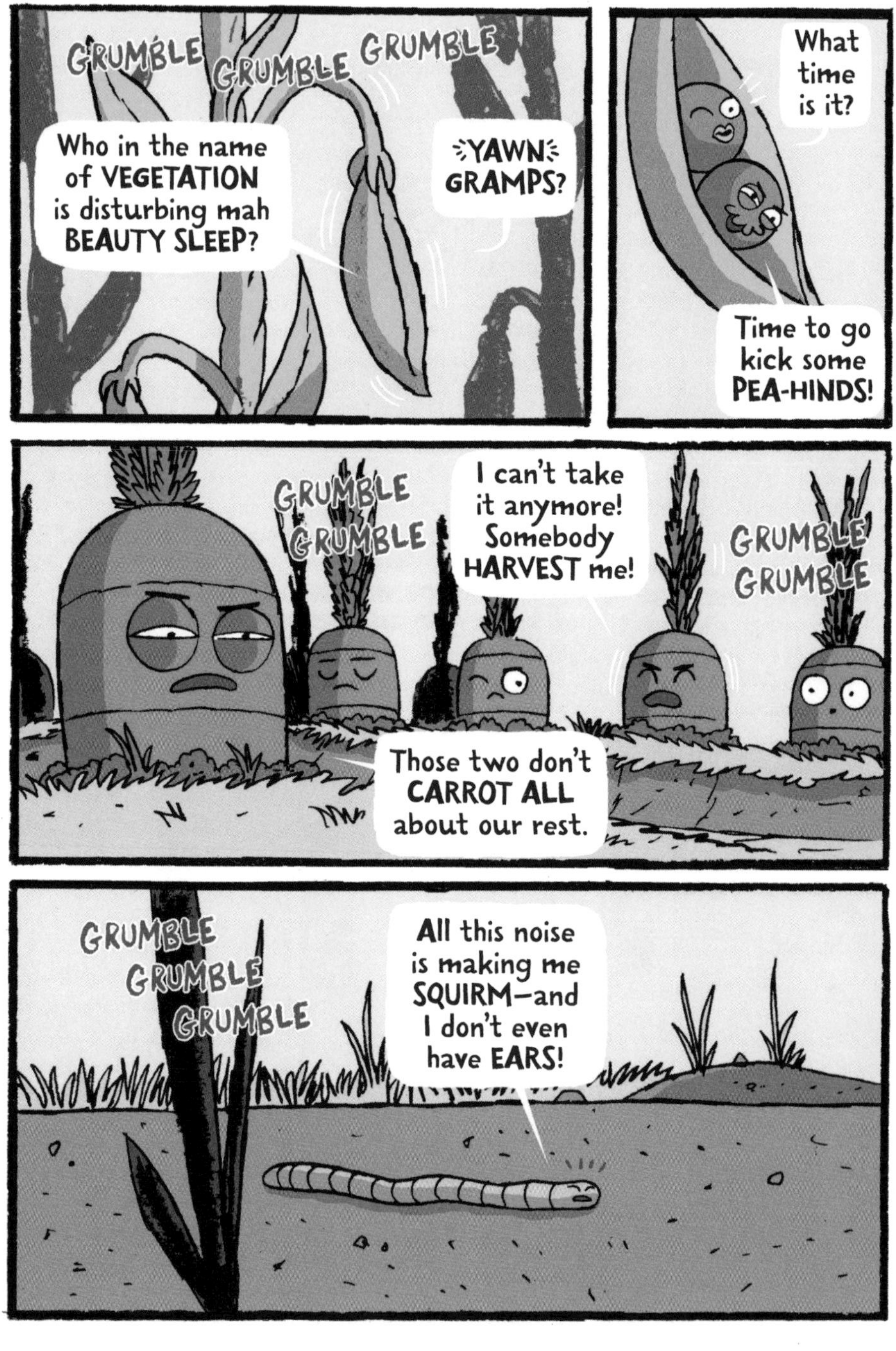
GRUMBLE GRUMBLE GRUMBLE
Who in the name of VEGETATION is disturbing mah BEAUTY SLEEP?
YAWN GRAMPS?
What time is it?
Time to go kick some PEA-HINDS!
GRUMBLE GRUMBLE
I can't take it anymore! Somebody HARVEST me!
GRUMBLE GRUMBLE
Those two don't CARROT ALL about our rest.
GRUMBLE GRUMBLE GRUMBLE
All this noise is making me SQUIRM—and I don't even have EARS!

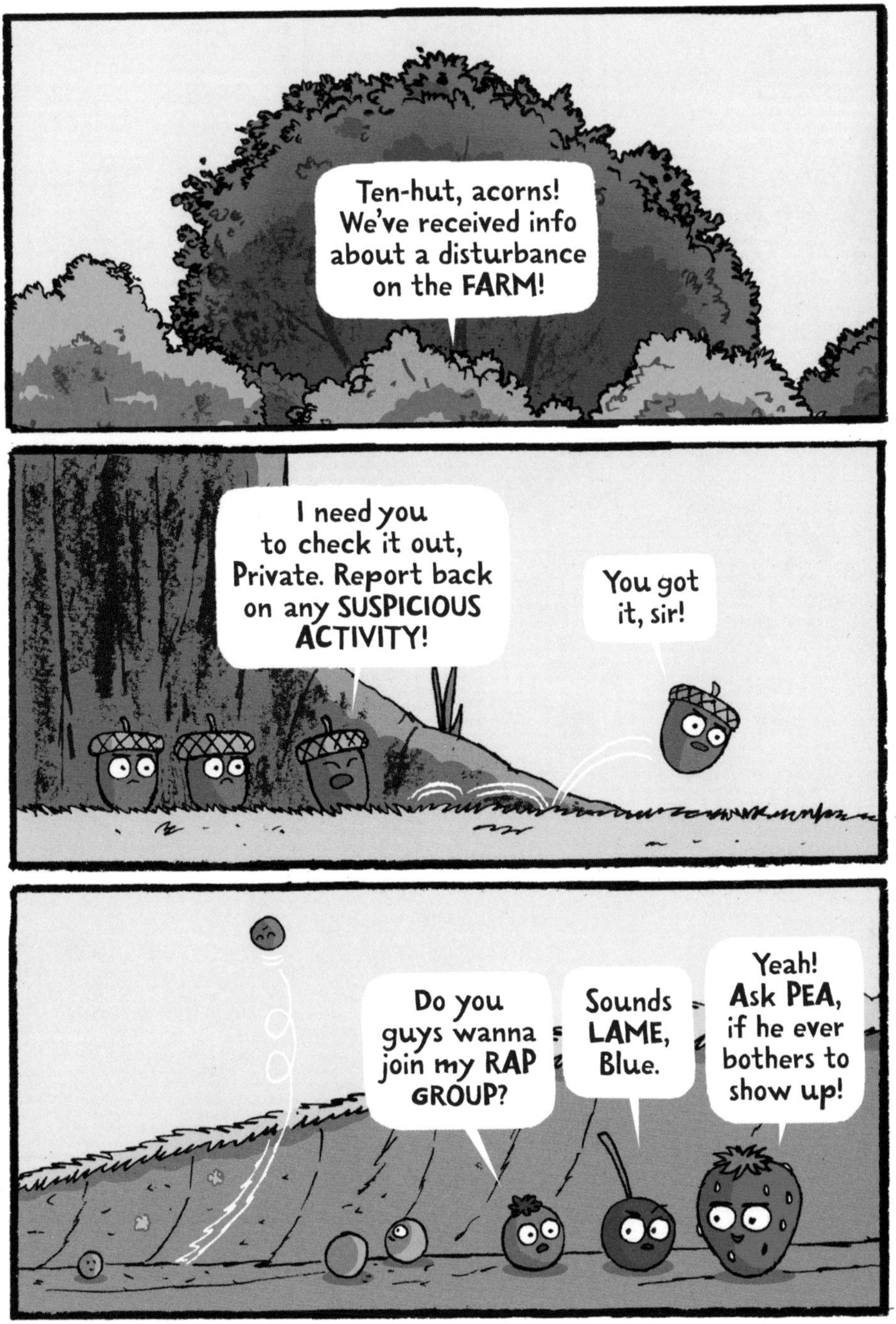

Ten-hut, acorns! We've received info about a disturbance on the FARM!
I need you to check it out, Private. Report back on any SUSPICIOUS ACTIVITY!
You got it, sir!
Do you guys wanna join my RAP GROUP?
Sounds LAME, Blue.
Yeah! Ask PEA, if he ever bothers to show up!

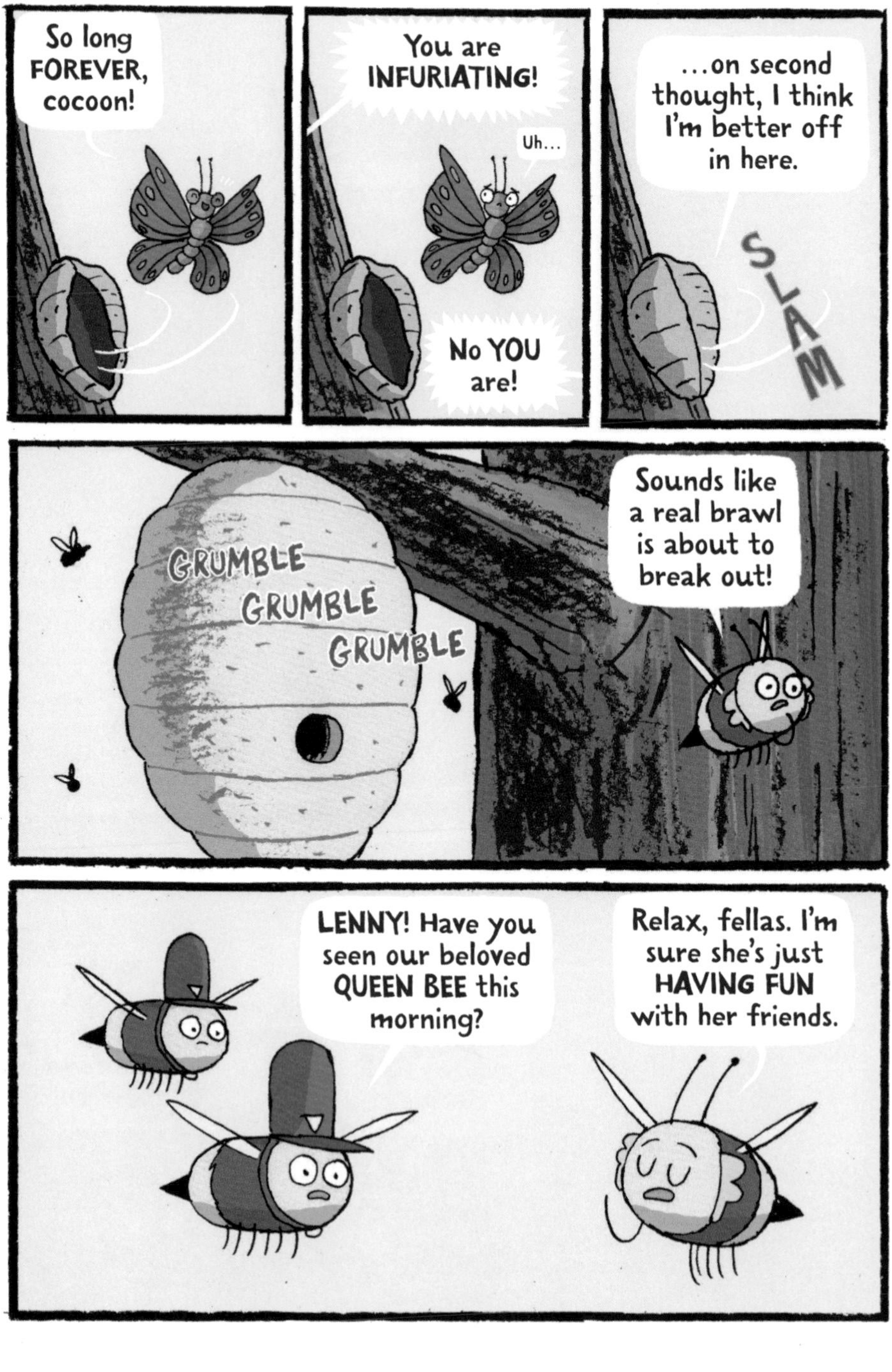
So long FOREVER, cocoon!
You are INFURIATING!
Uh...
No YOU are!
...on second thought, I think I'm better off in here.
SLAM
GRUMBLE
GRUMBLE
GRUMBLE
Sounds like a real brawl is about to break out!
LENNY! Have you seen our beloved QUEEN BEE this morning?
Relax, fellas. I'm sure she's just HAVING FUN with her friends.

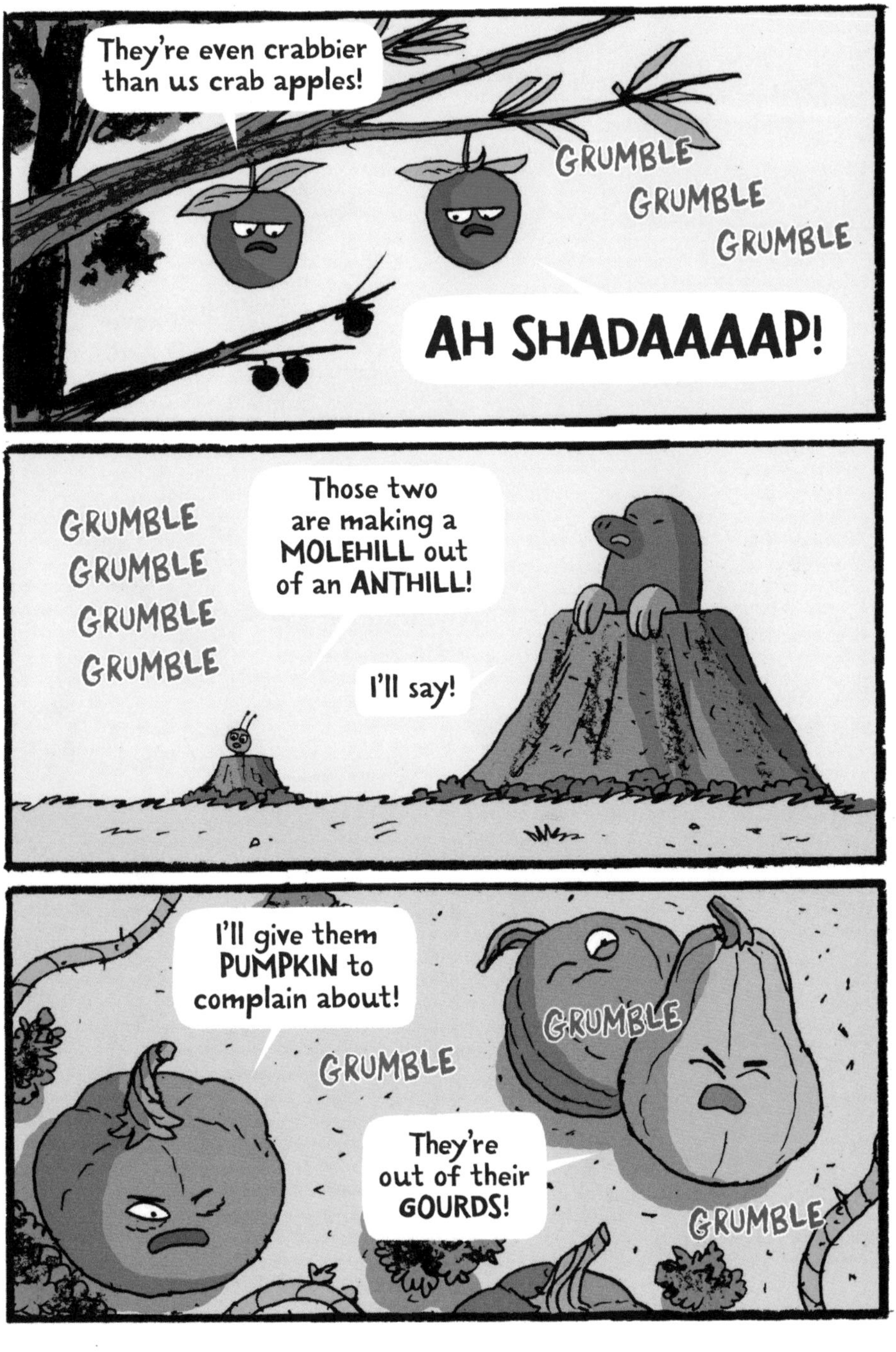

They're even crabbier than us crab apples!
GRUMBLE
GRUMBLE
GRUMBLE
AH SHADAAAAP!
GRUMBLE
GRUMBLE
GRUMBLE
GRUMBLE
Those two are making a MOLEHILL out of an ANTHILL!
I'll say!
I'll give them PUMPKIN to complain about!
GRUMBLE
GRUMBLE
They're out of their GOURDS!
GRUMBLE

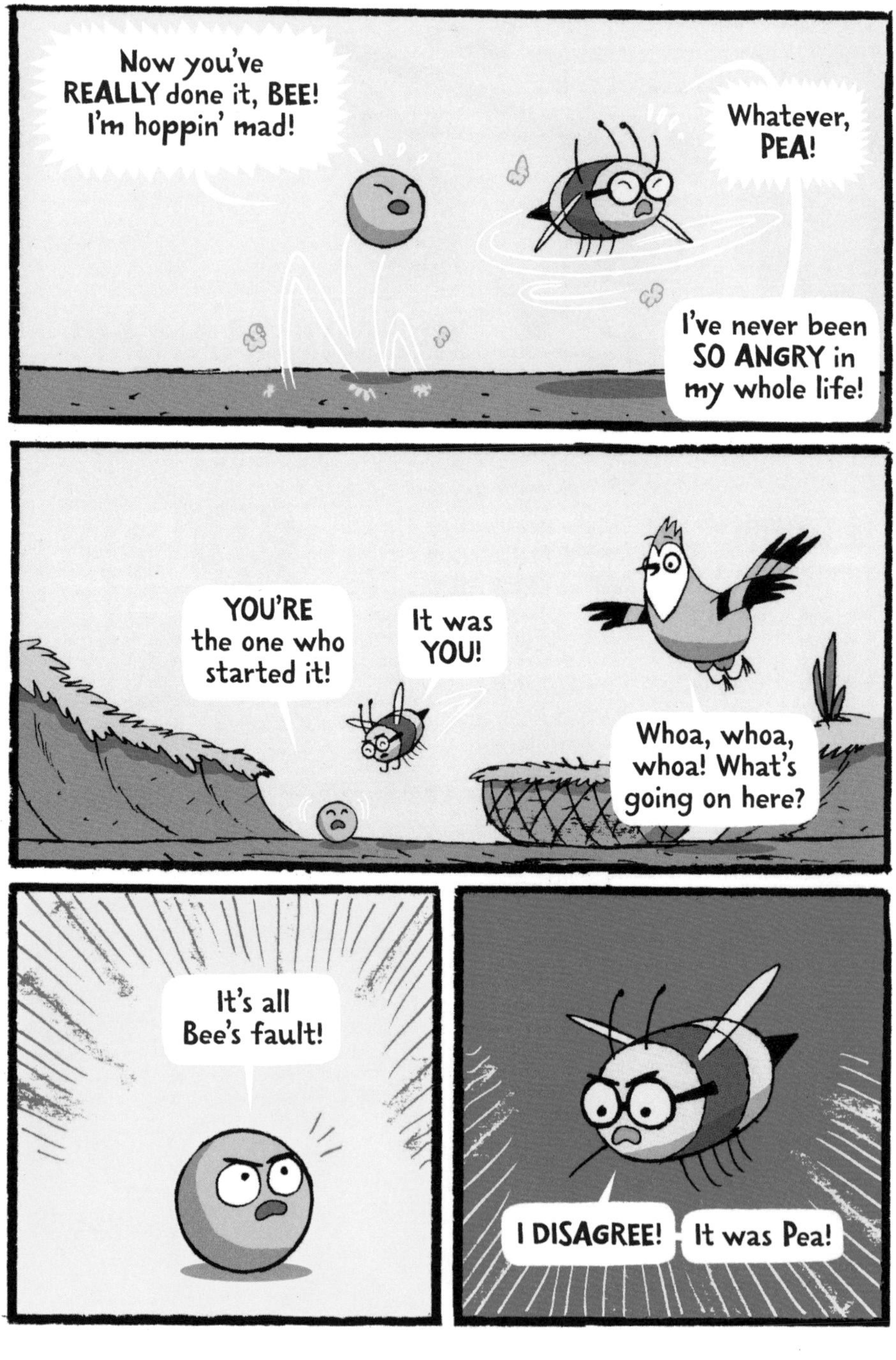
Now you've REALLY done it, BEE! I'm hoppin' mad!
Whatever, PEA!
I've never been SO ANGRY in my whole life!
YOU'RE the one who started it!
It was YOU!
Whoa, whoa, whoa! What's going on here?
It's all Bee's fault!
I DISAGREE!
It was Pea!

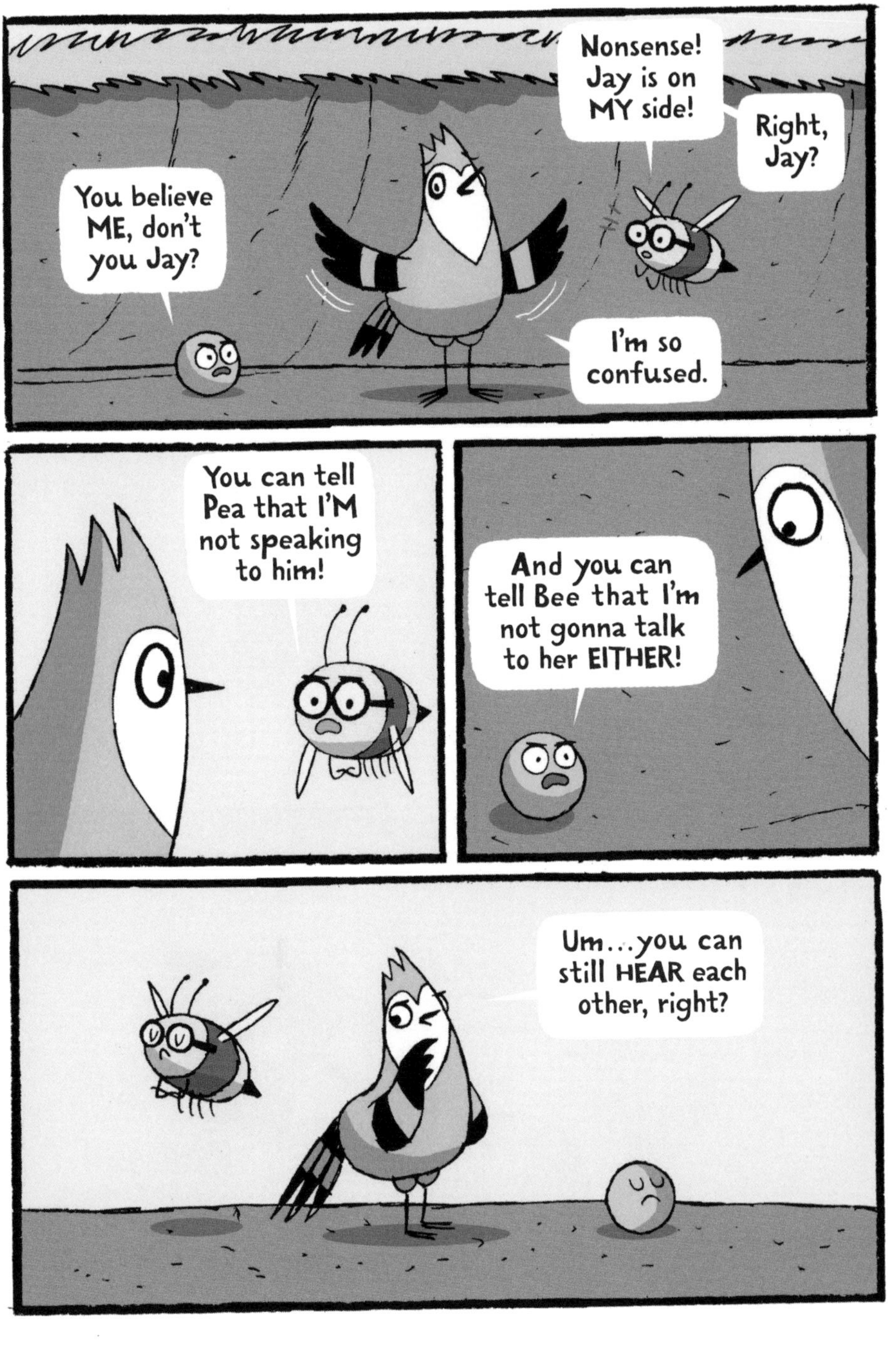
You believe ME, don't you Jay?
Nonsense! Jay is on MY side!
Right, Jay?
I'm so confused.
You can tell Pea that I'M not speaking to him!
And you can tell Bee that I'm not gonna talk to her EITHER!
Um...you can still HEAR each other, right?

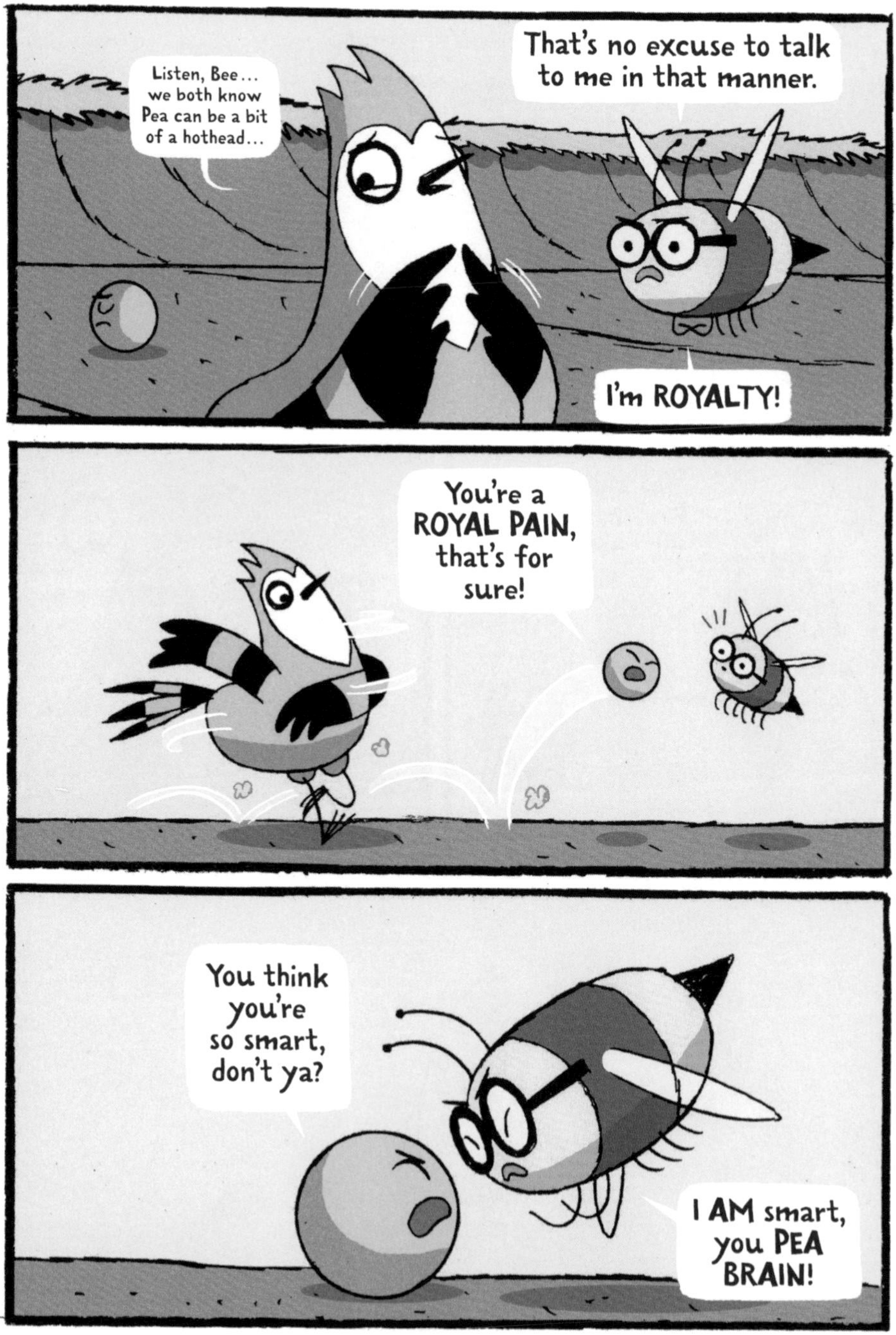
Listen, Bee... we both know Pea can be a bit of a hothead...
That's no excuse to talk to me in that manner.
I'm ROYALTY!
You're a ROYAL PAIN, that's for sure!
You think you're so smart, don't ya?
I AM smart, you PEA BRAIN!

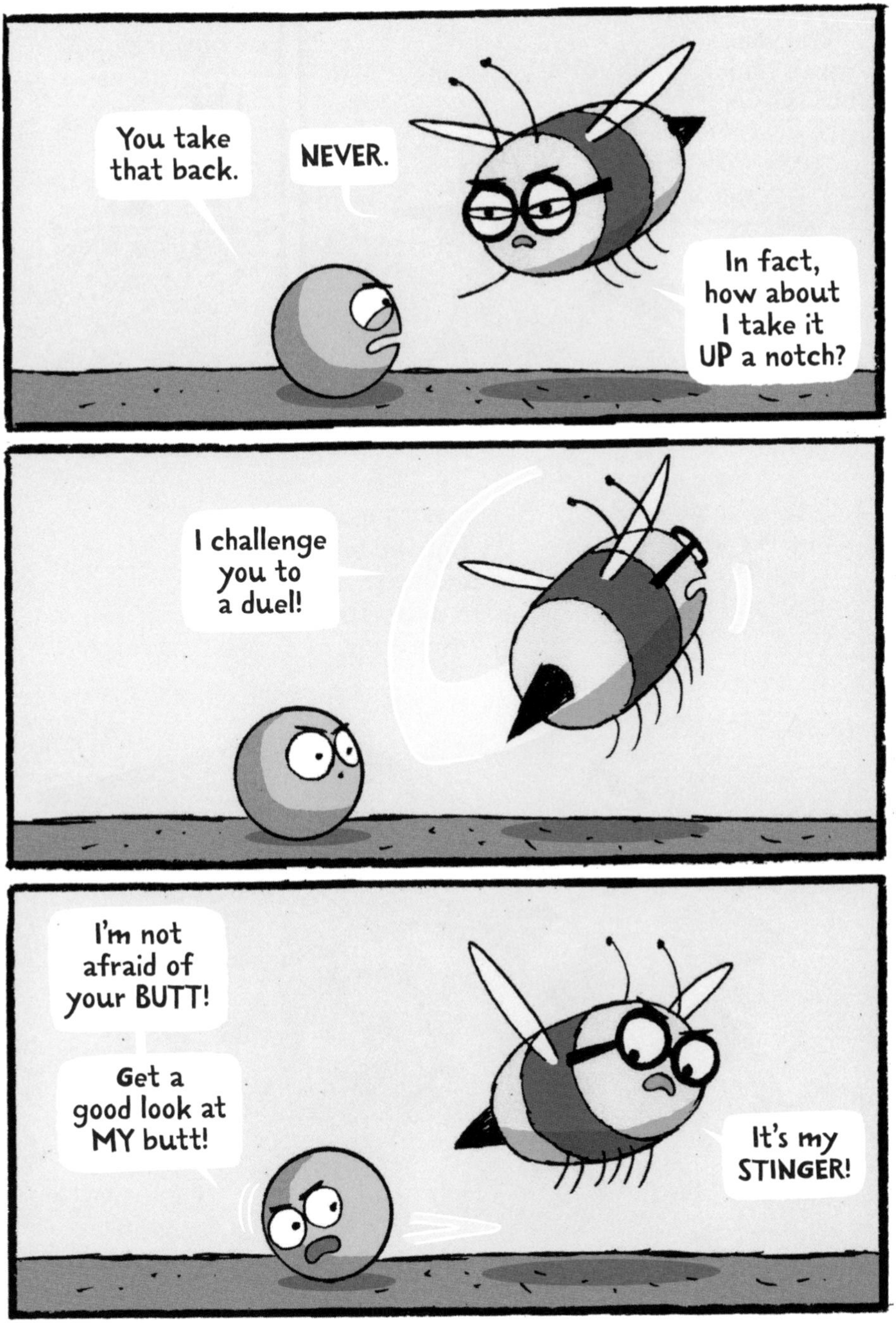
You take that back.
NEVER.
In fact, how about I take it UP a notch?
I challenge you to a duel!
I'm not afraid of your BUTT!
Get a good look at MY butt!
It's my STINGER!

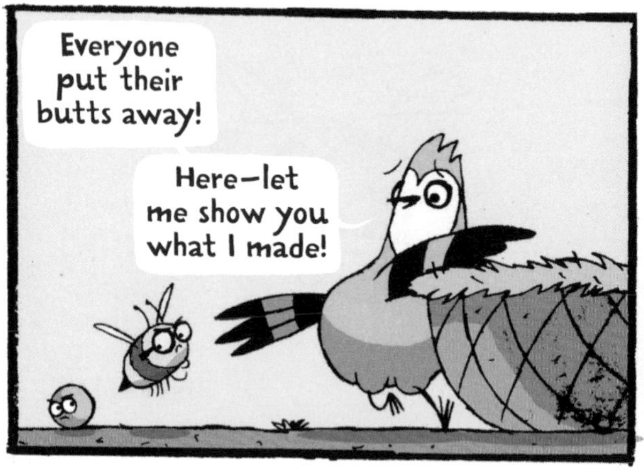
Everyone put their butts away!
Here—let me show you what I made!

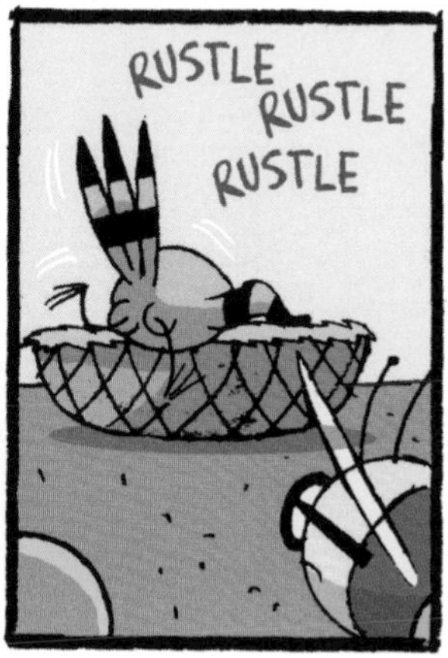
RUSTLE
RUSTLE
RUSTLE

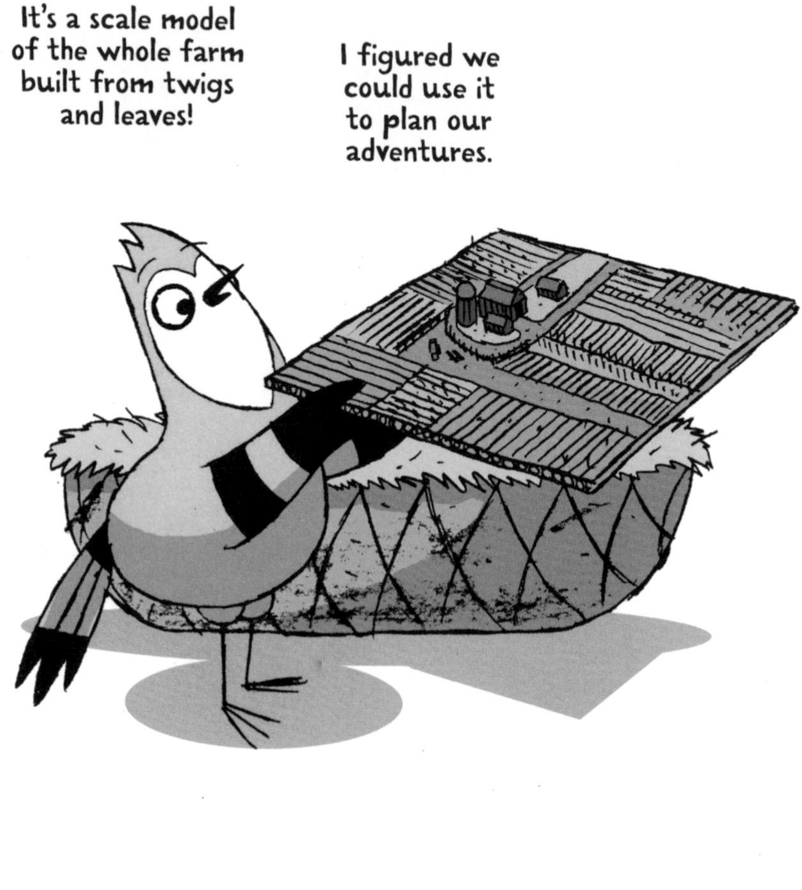
It's a scale model of the whole farm built from twigs and leaves!
I figured we could use it to plan our adventures.

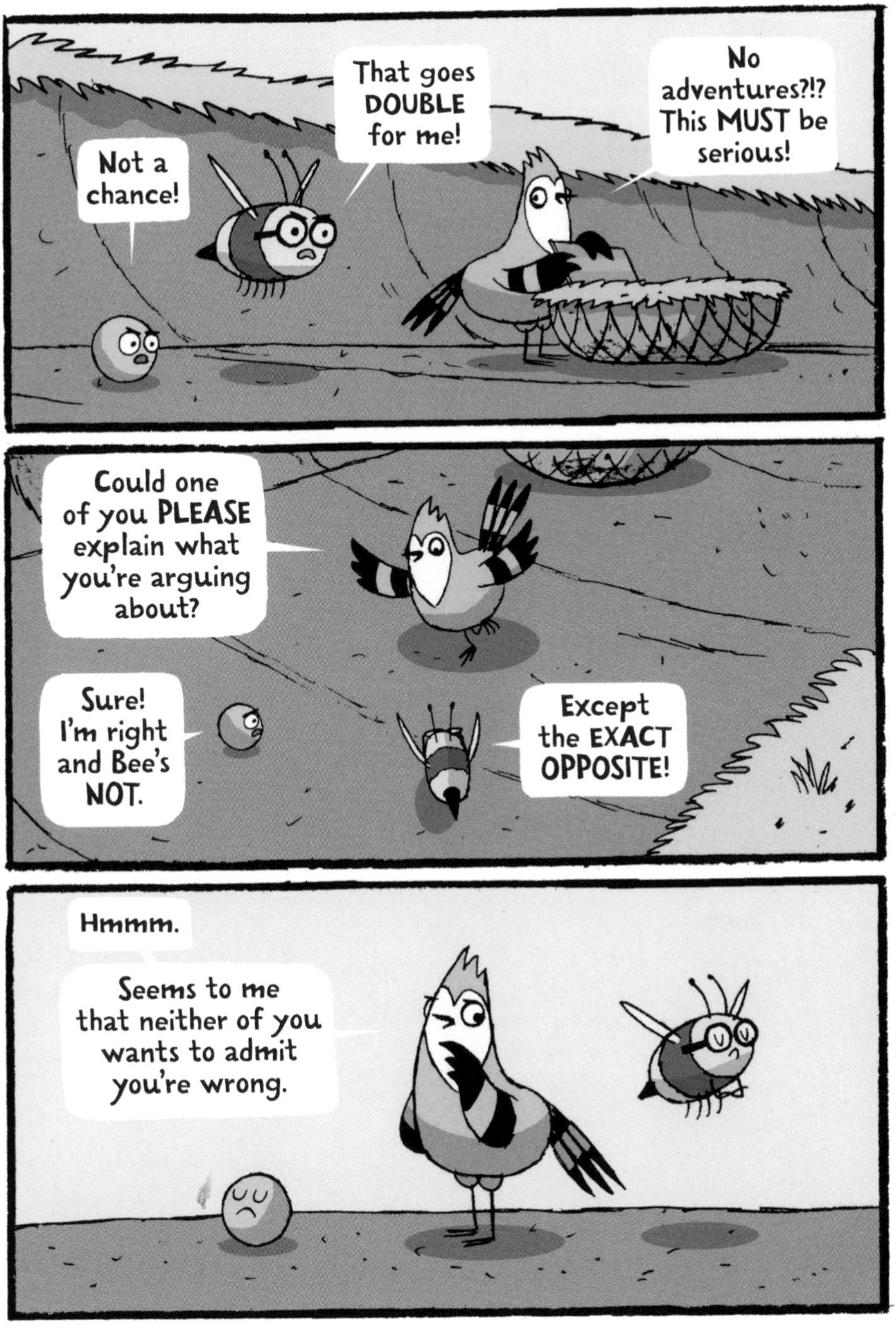
Not a chance!
That goes DOUBLE for me!
No adventures?!? This MUST be serious!
Could one of you PLEASE explain what you're arguing about?
Sure! I'm right and Bee's NOT.
Except the EXACT OPPOSITE!
Hmmm.
Seems to me that neither of you wants to admit you're wrong.

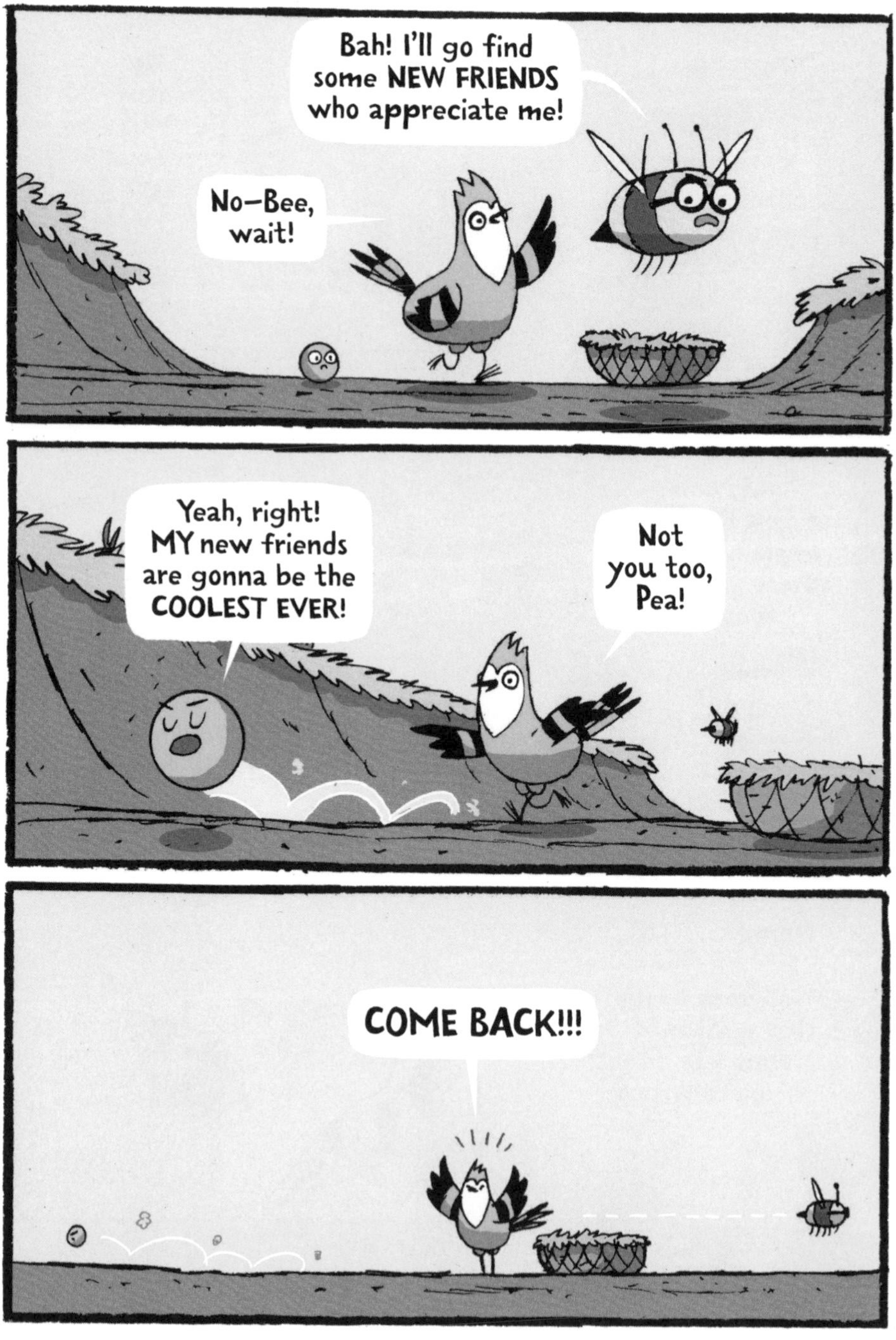
Bah! I'll go find some NEW FRIENDS who appreciate me!
No-Bee, wait!
Yeah, right! MY new friends are gonna be the COOLEST EVER!
Not you too, Pea!
COME BACK!!!

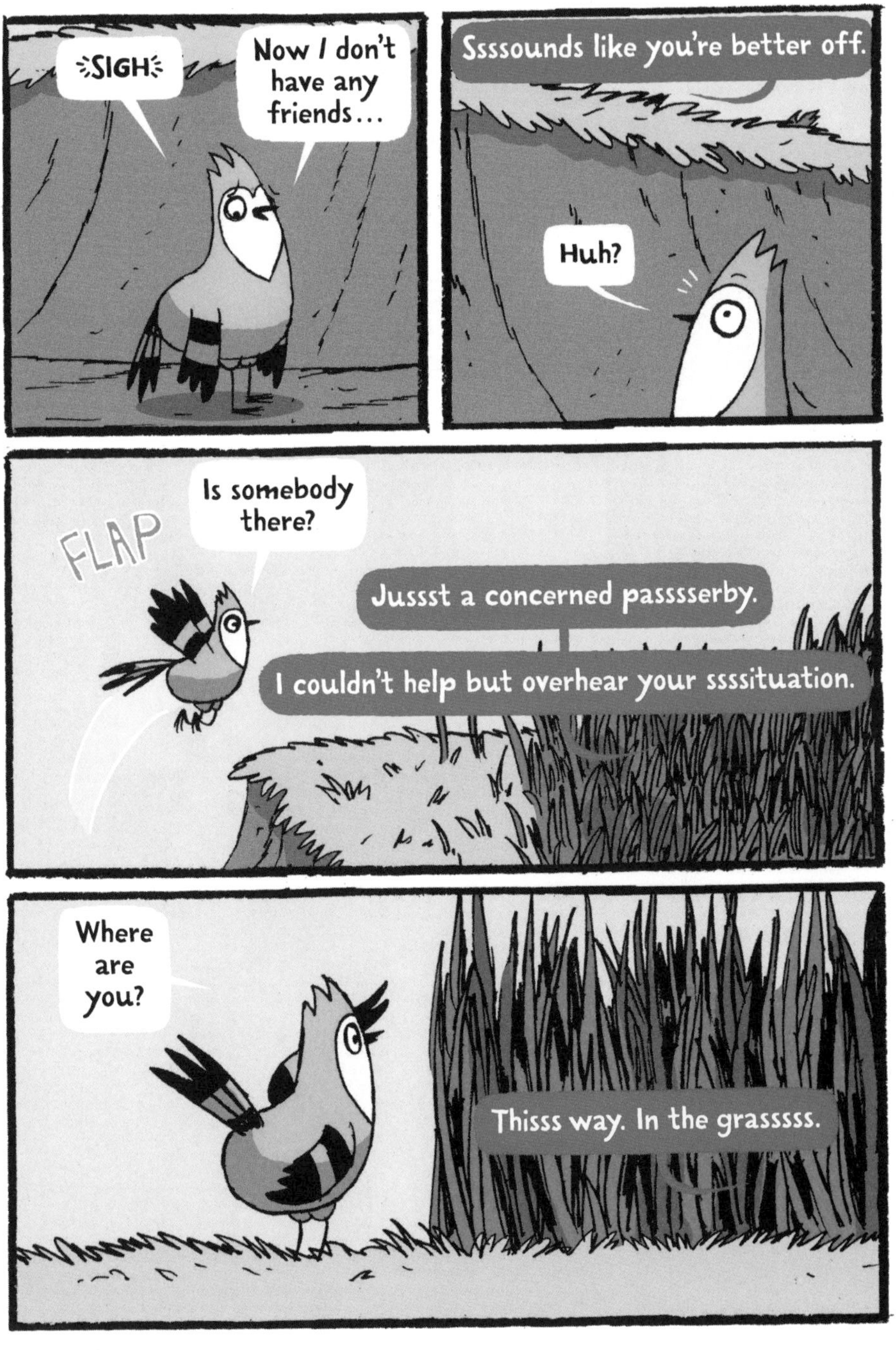
SIGH
Now I don't have any friends...
Ssssounds like you're better off.
Huh?
FLAP
Is somebody there?
Jussst a concerned passsserby.
I couldn't help but overhear your ssssituation.
Where are you?
Thisss way. In the grasssss.

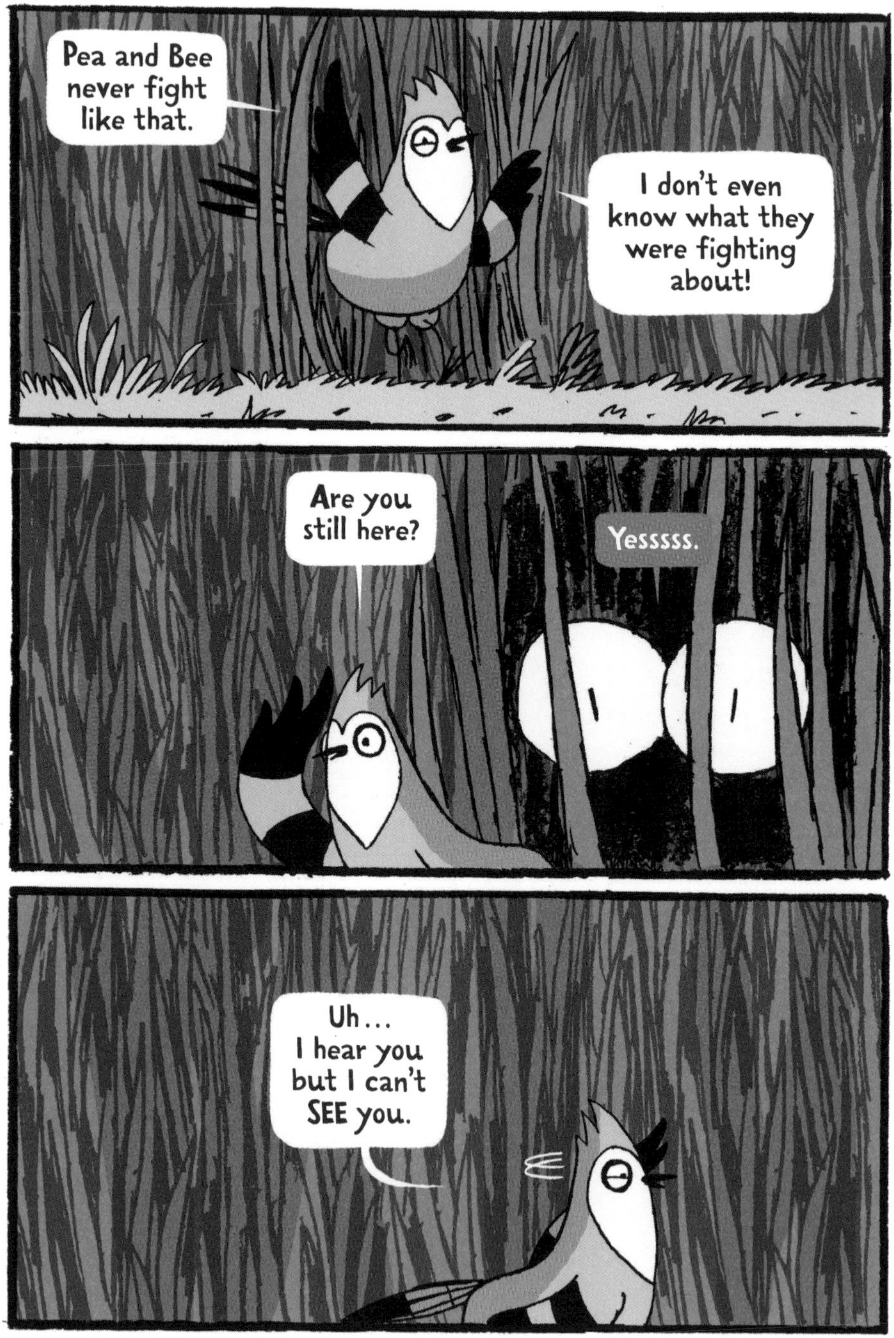
Pea and Bee never fight like that.
I don't even know what they were fighting about!
Are you still here?
Yesssss.
Uh...
I hear you but I can't SEE you.

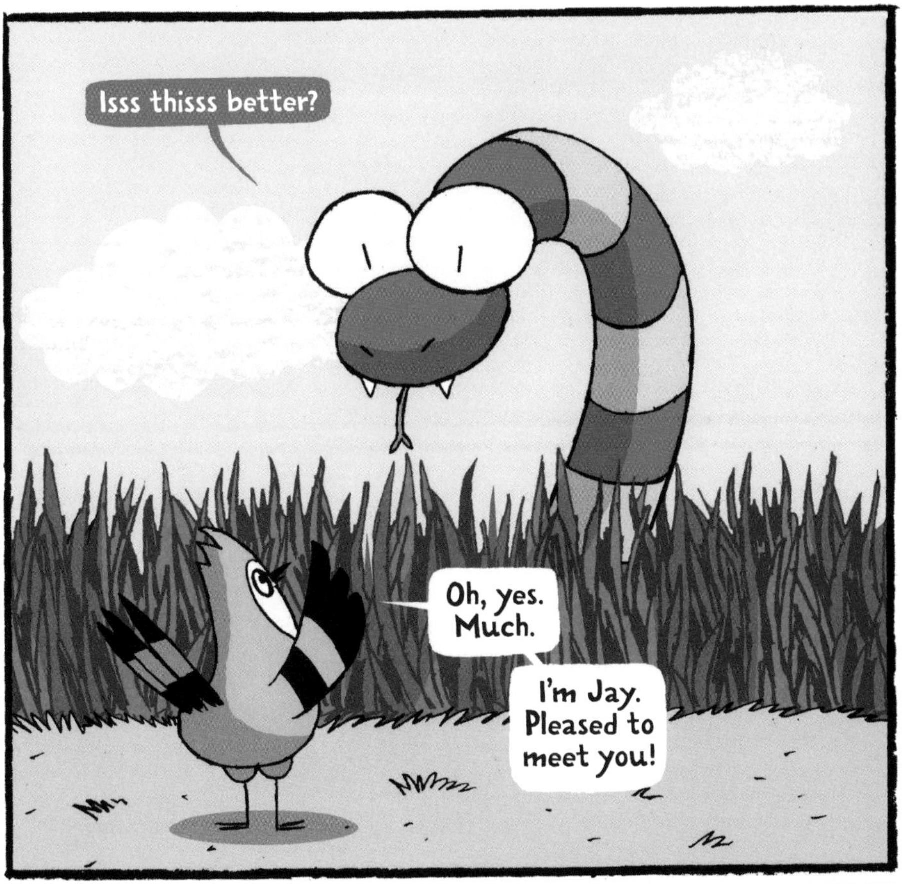
Isss thisss better?
Oh, yes. Much.
I'm Jay. Pleased to meet you!

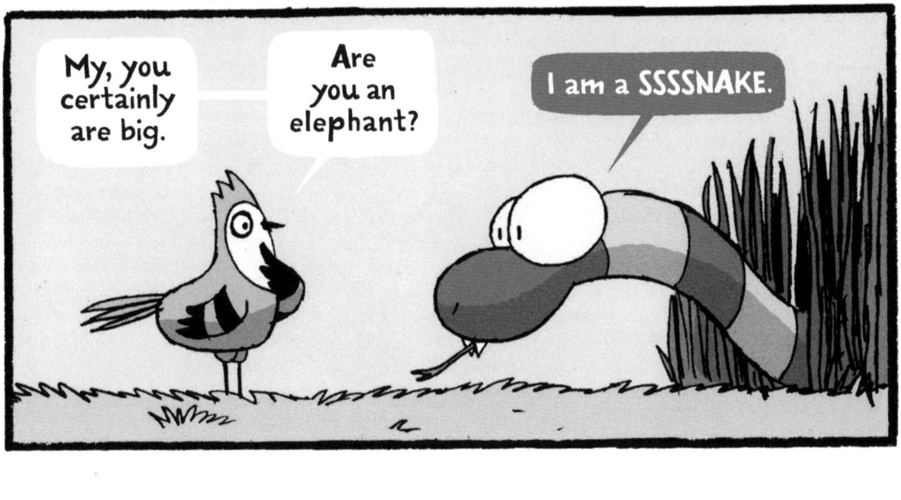
My, you certainly are big.
Are you an elephant?
I am a SSSSNAKE.

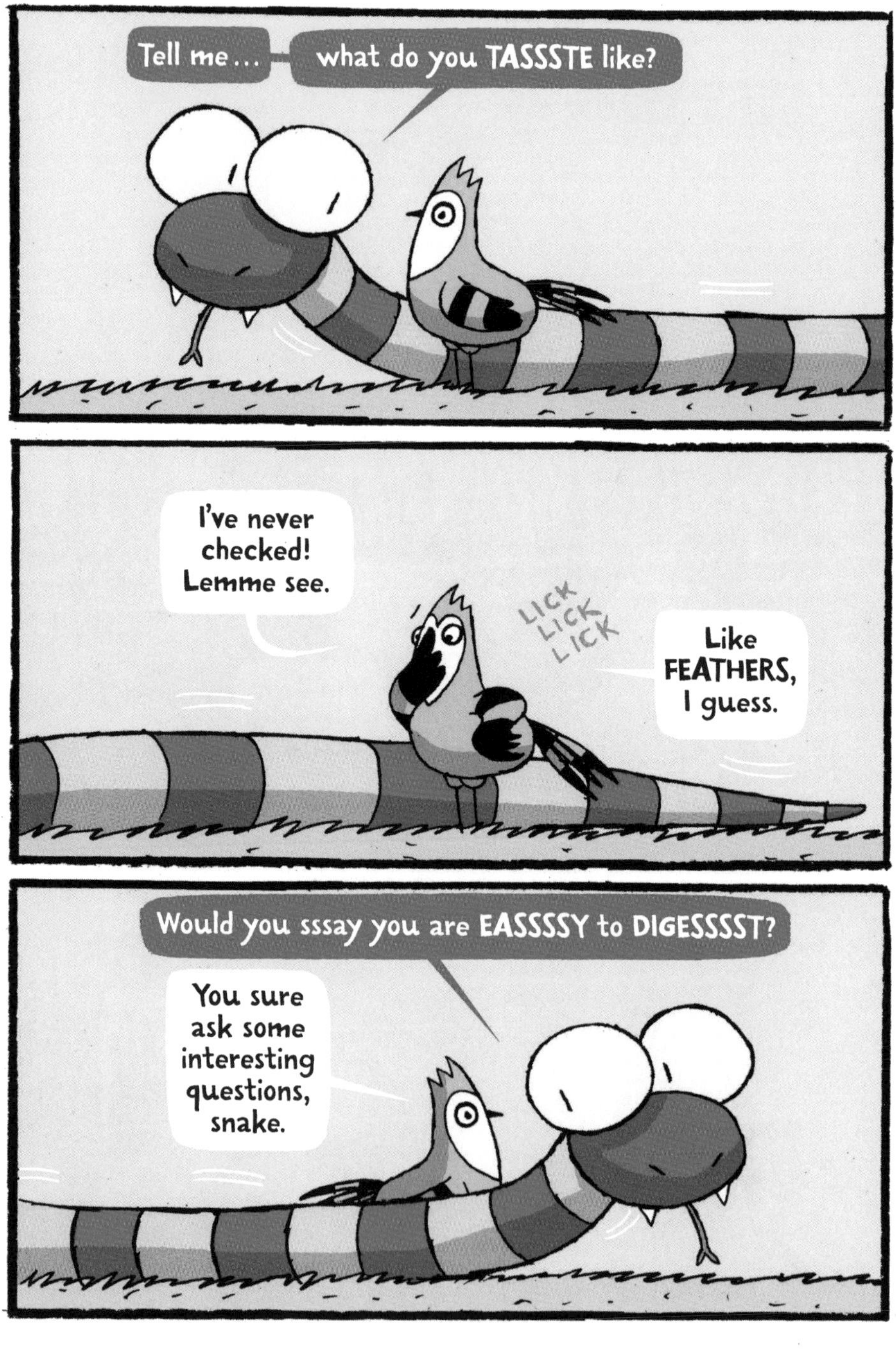

Tell me...
what do you TASSSTE like?
I've never checked! Lemme see.
LICK LICK LICK
Like FEATHERS, I guess.
Would you sssay you are EASSSSY to DIGESSSST?
You sure ask some interesting questions, snake.

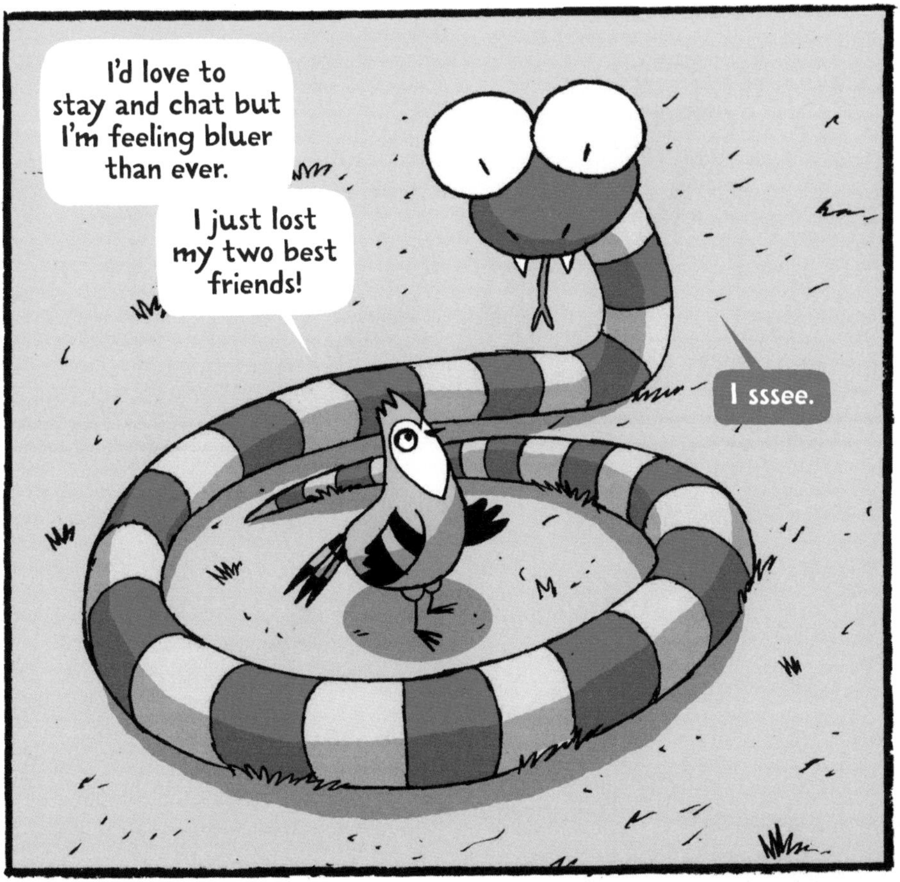
I'd love to stay and chat but I'm feeling bluer than ever.
I just lost my two best friends!
I sssee.

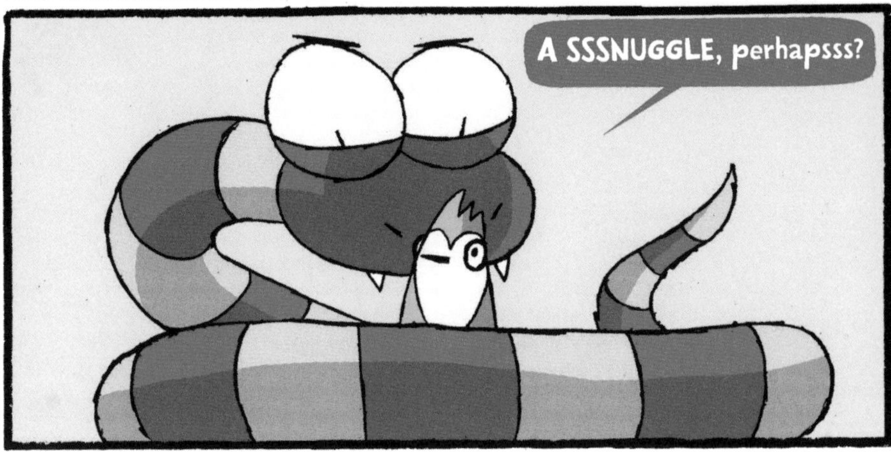
A SSSNUGGLE, perhapsss?

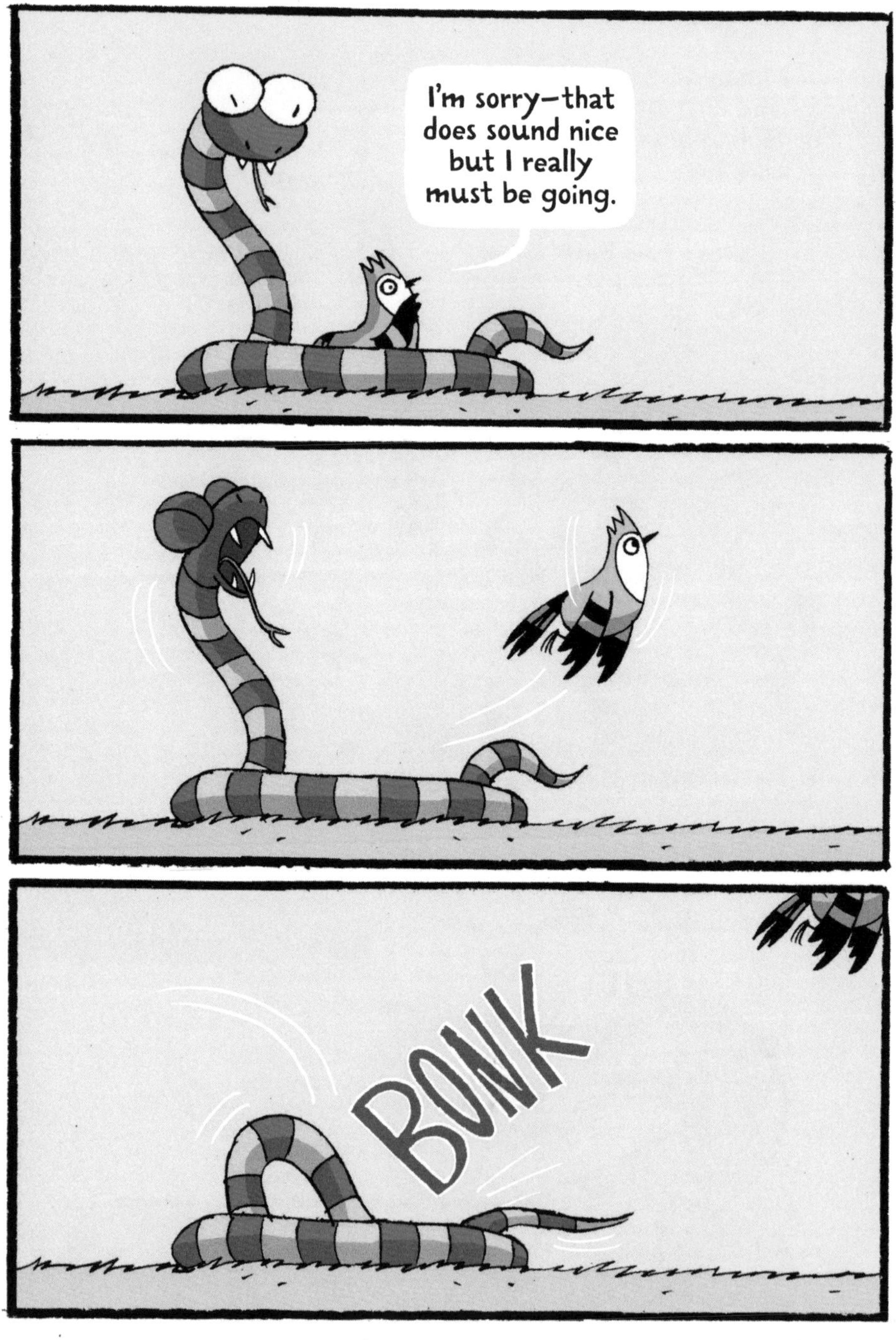
I'm sorry—that does sound nice but I really must be going.
BONK

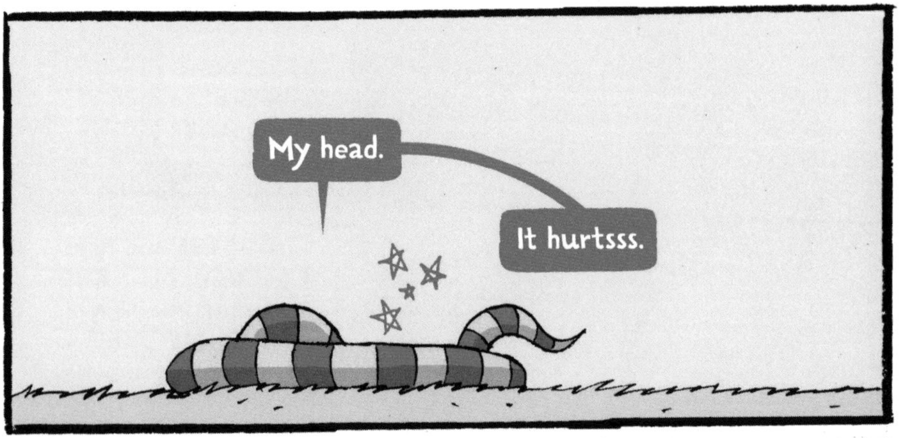
My head.
It hurtsss.

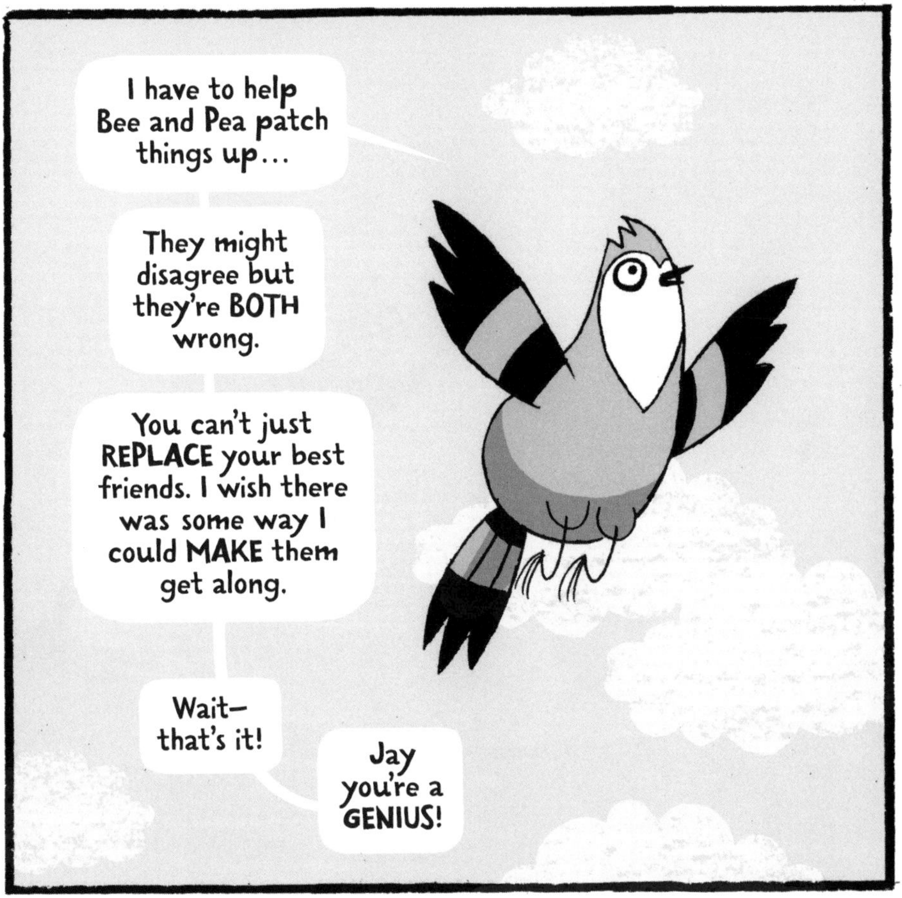
I have to help Bee and Pea patch things up…
They might disagree but they're BOTH wrong.
You can't just REPLACE your best friends. I wish there was some way I could MAKE them get along.
Wait— that's it!
Jay you're a GENIUS!

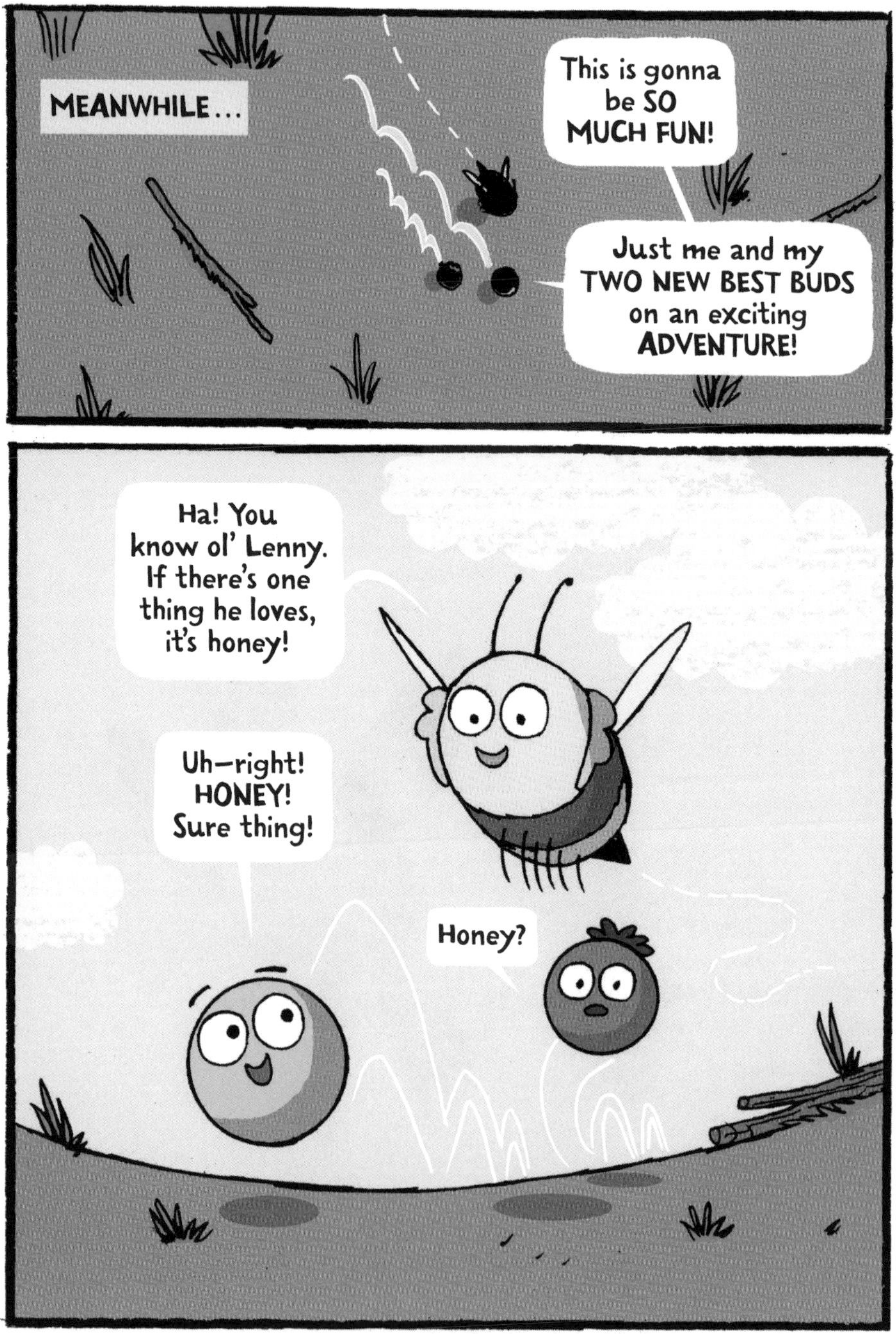
MEANWHILE...
This is gonna be SO MUCH FUN!
Just me and my TWO NEW BEST BUDS on an exciting ADVENTURE!
Ha! You know ol' Lenny. If there's one thing he loves, it's honey!
Uh—right! HONEY! Sure thing!
Honey?

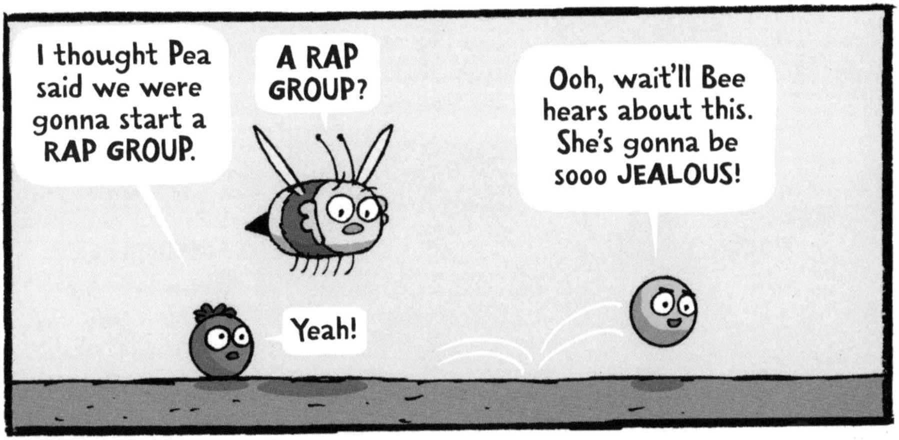
I thought Pea said we were gonna start a **RAP GROUP.**
A RAP GROUP?
Ooh, wait'll Bee hears about this. She's gonna be sooo **JEALOUS!**
Yeah!

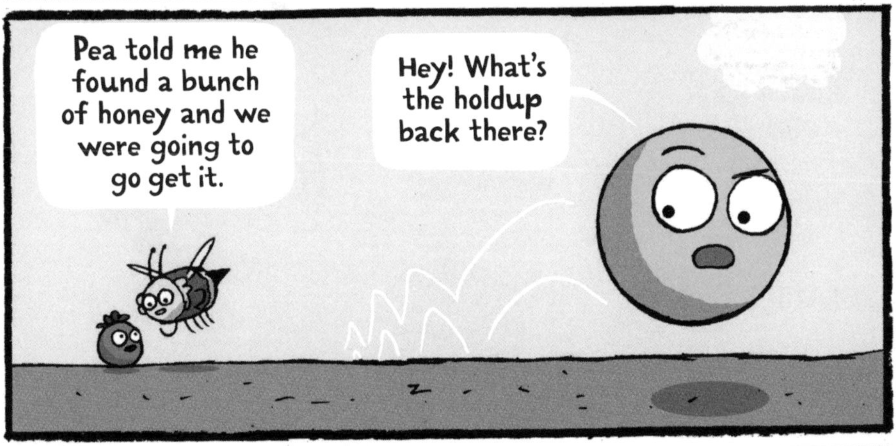
Pea told me he found a bunch of honey and we were going to go get it.
Hey! What's the holdup back there?

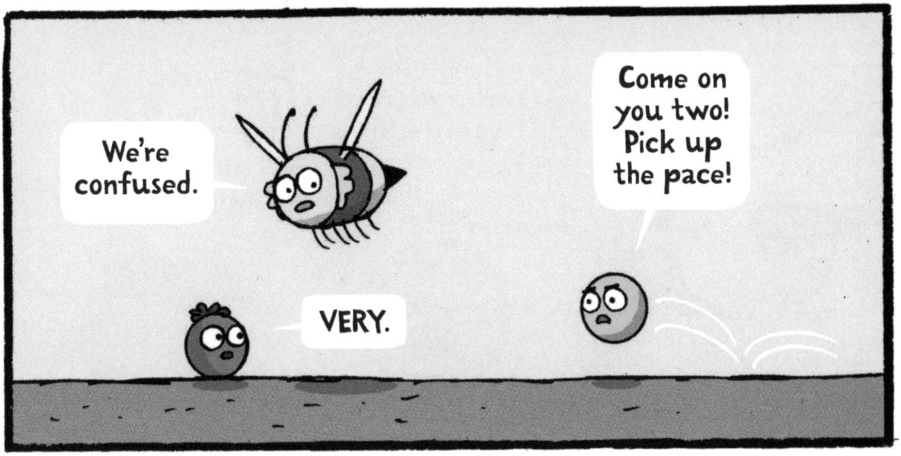
We're confused.
VERY.
Come on you two! Pick up the pace!

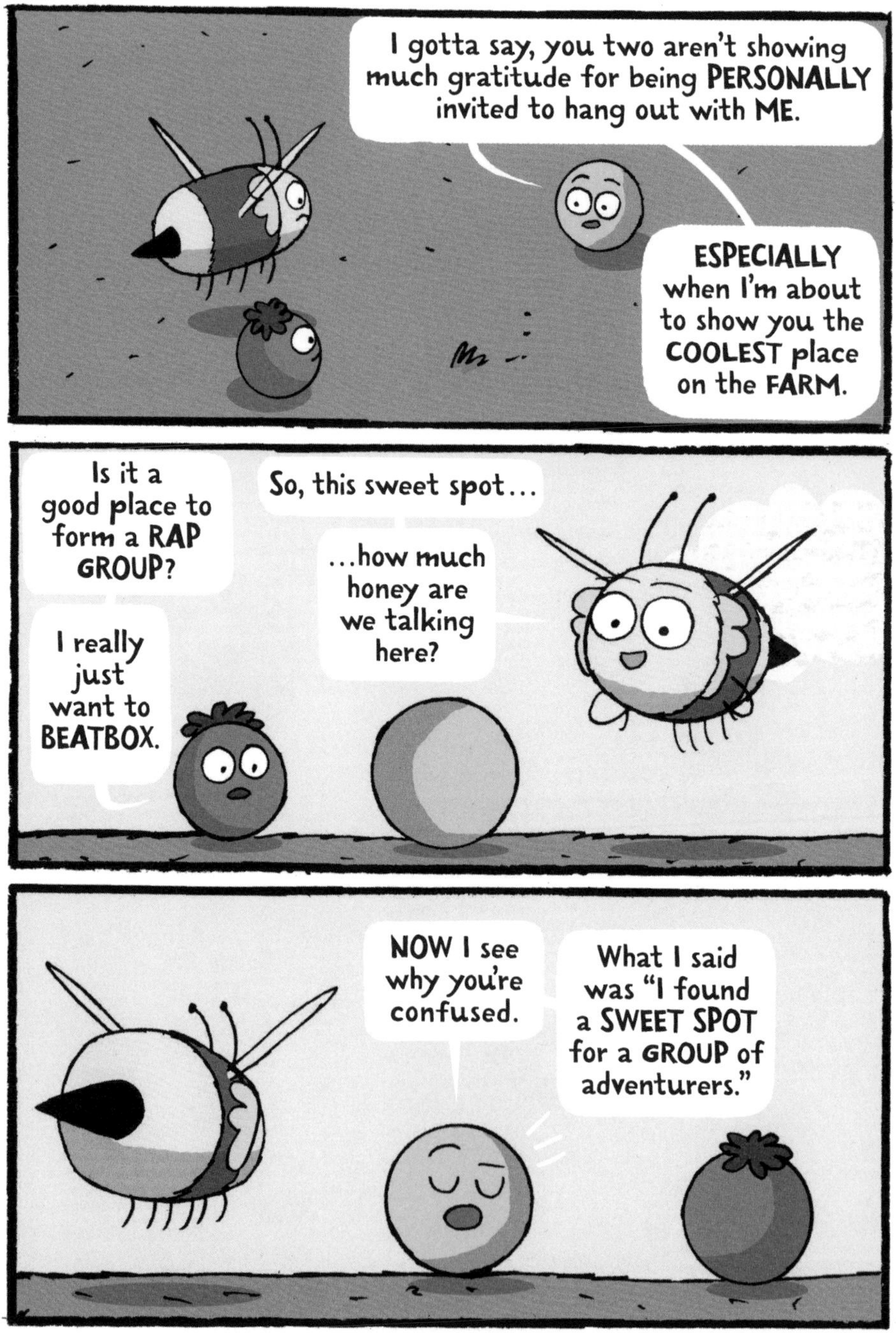
I gotta say, you two aren't showing much gratitude for being PERSONALLY invited to hang out with ME.
ESPECIALLY when I'm about to show you the COOLEST place on the FARM.
Is it a good place to form a RAP GROUP?
I really just want to BEATBOX.
So, this sweet spot...
...how much honey are we talking here?
NOW I see why you're confused.
What I said was "I found a SWEET SPOT for a GROUP of adventurers."

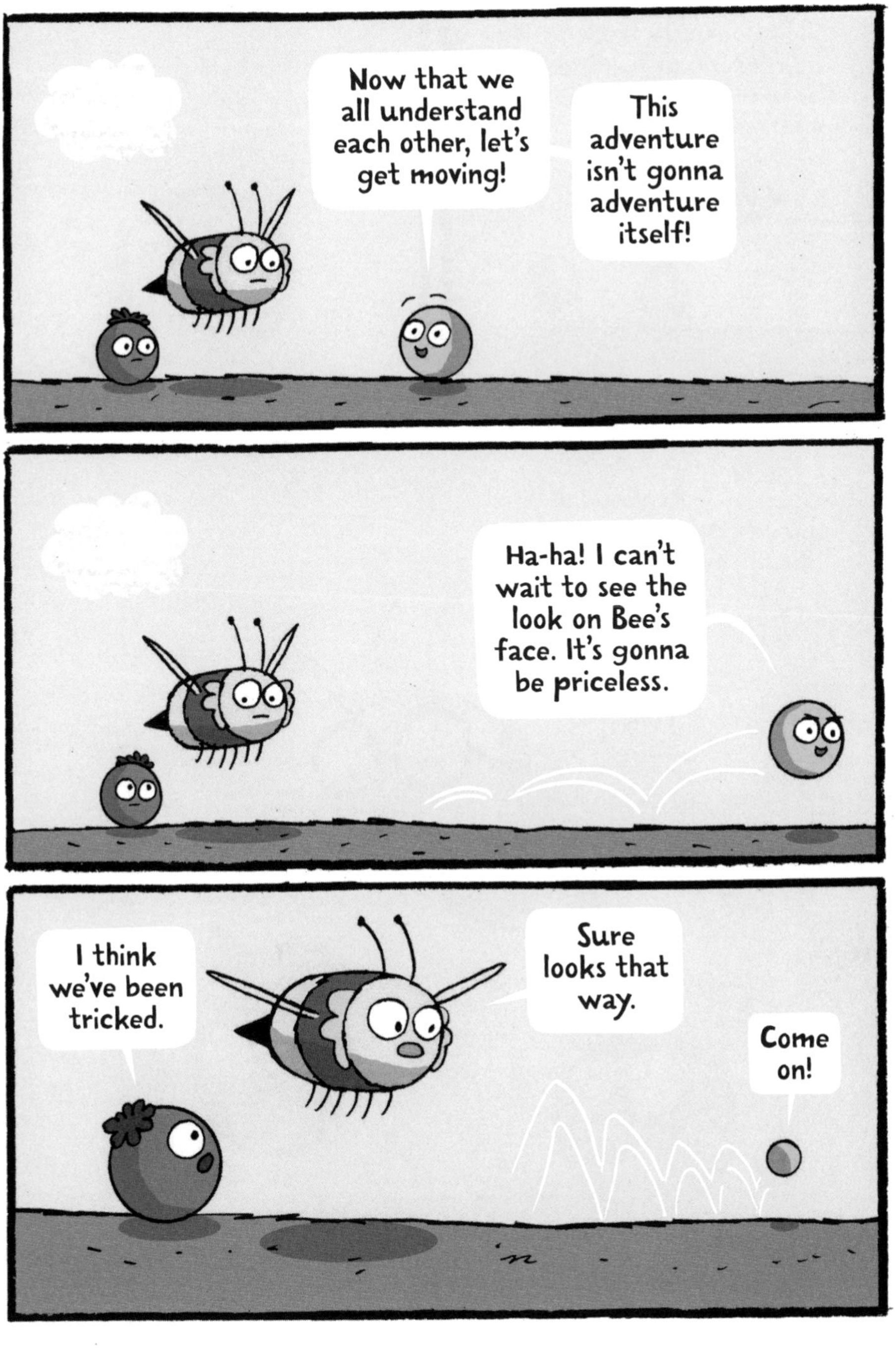
Now that we all understand each other, let's get moving!
This adventure isn't gonna adventure itself!
Ha-ha! I can't wait to see the look on Bee's face. It's gonna be priceless.
I think we've been tricked.
Sure looks that way.
Come on!

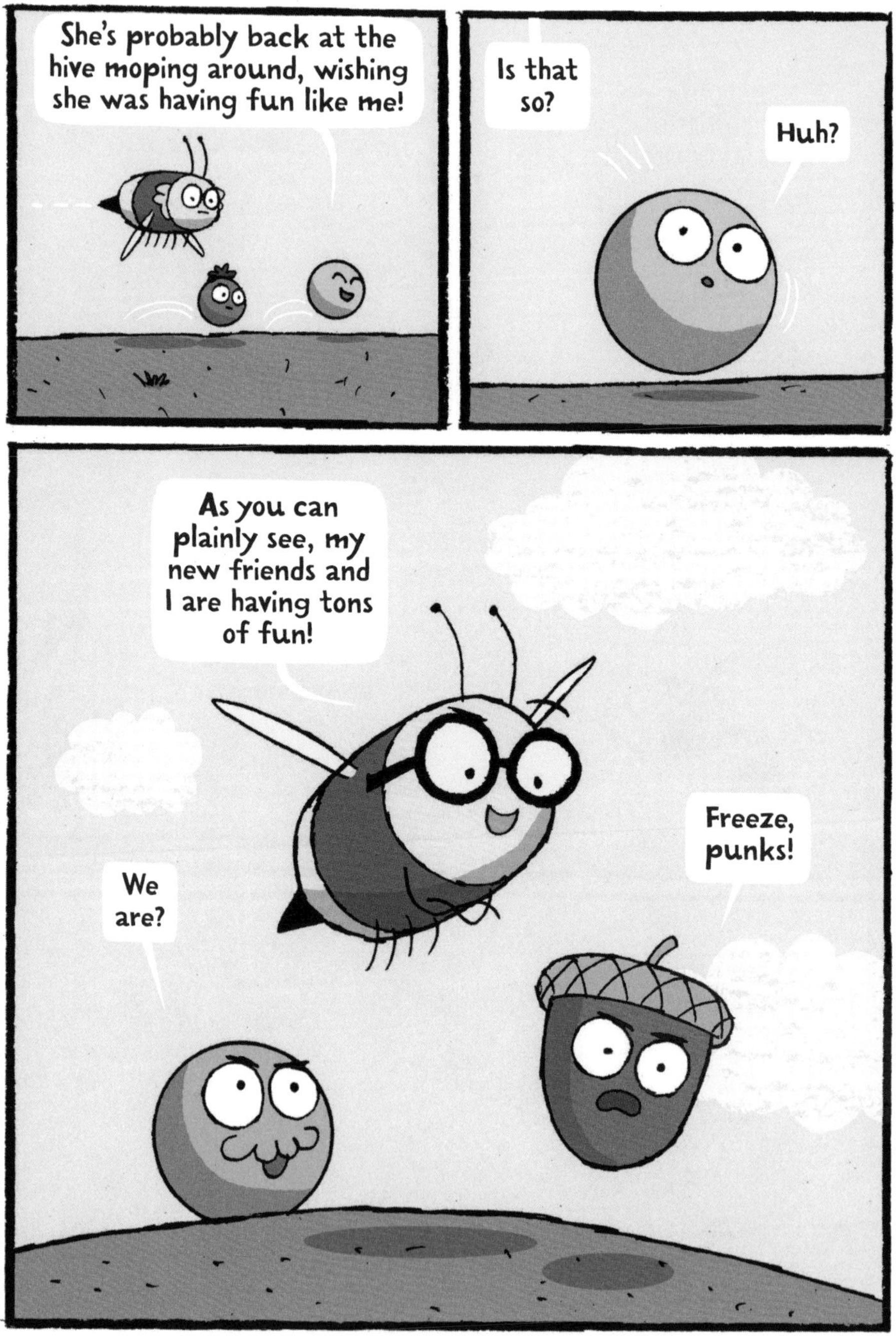
She's probably back at the hive moping around, wishing she was having fun like me!
Is that so?
Huh?
As you can plainly see, my new friends and I are having tons of fun!
We are?
Freeze, punks!

25

29

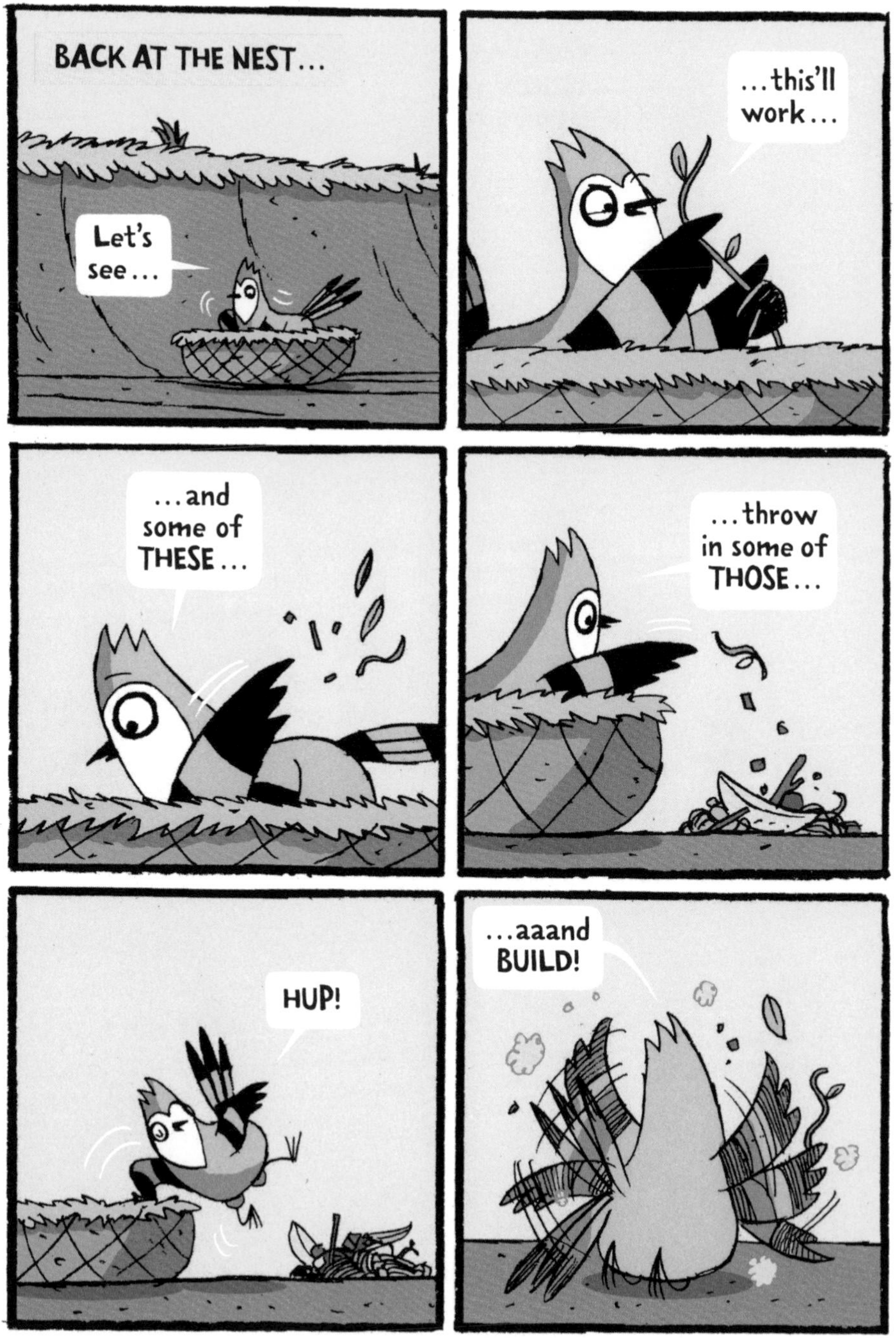
BACK AT THE NEST...
Let's see...
...this'll work...
...and some of THESE...
...throw in some of THOSE...
HUP!
...aaand BUILD!

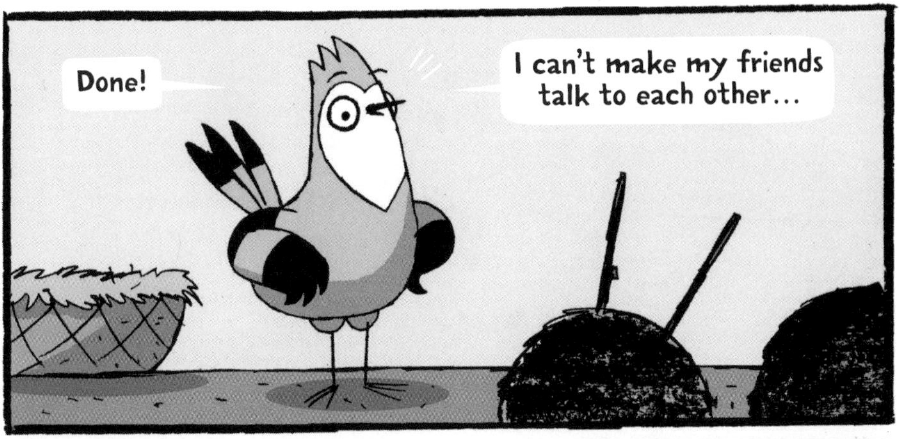
Done!
I can't make my friends talk to each other...

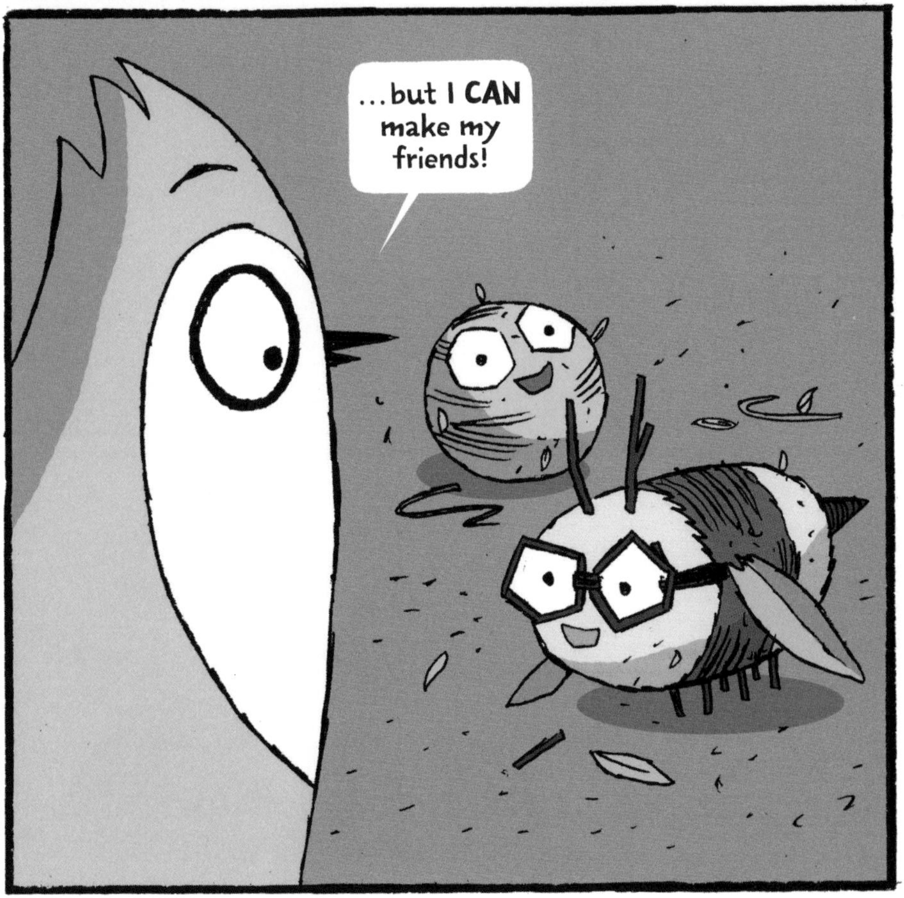
...but I **CAN** make my friends!

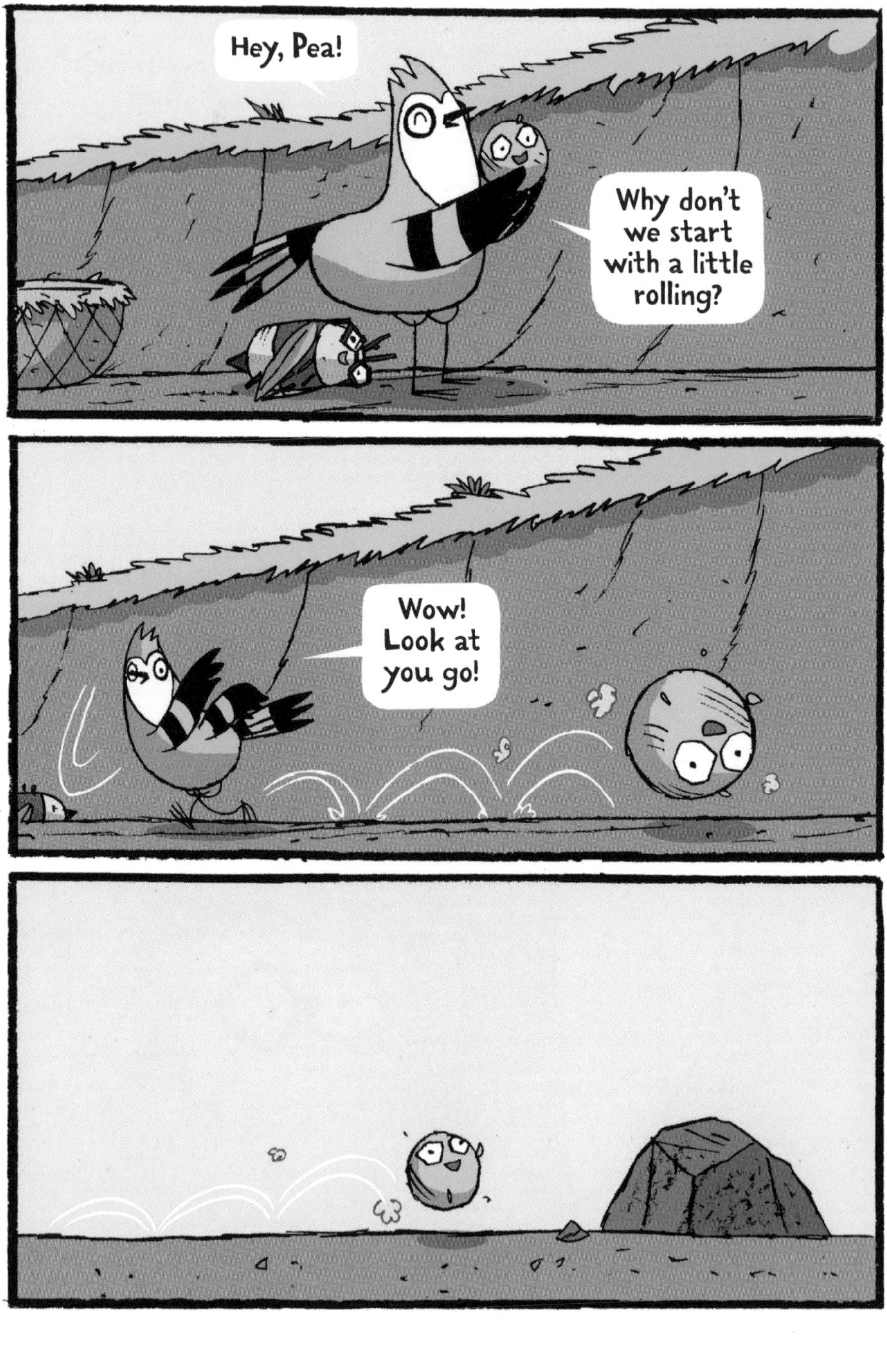
Hey, Pea!
Why don't we start with a little rolling?
Wow! Look at you go!

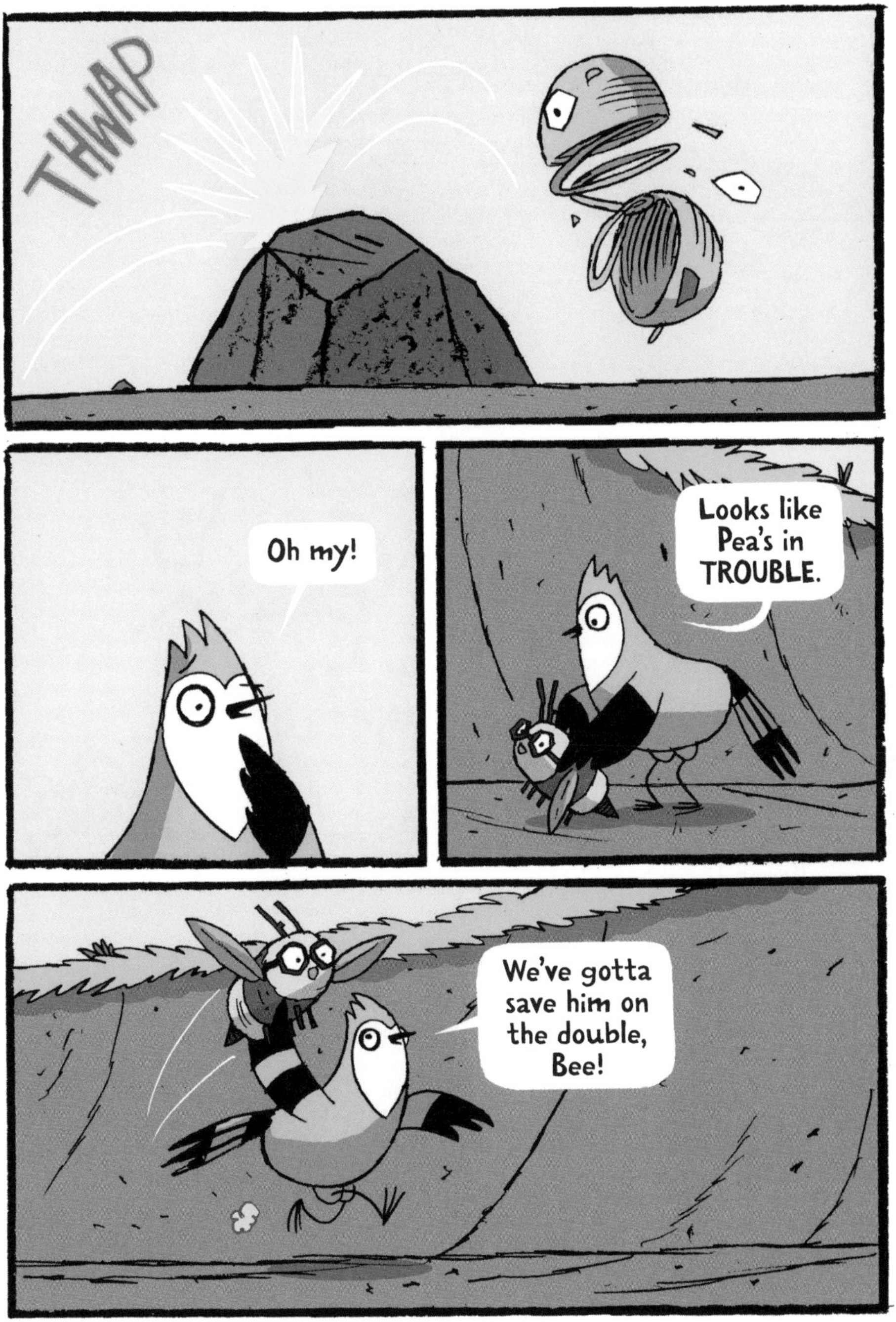
THWAP
Oh my!
Looks like Pea's in TROUBLE.
We've gotta save him on the double, Bee!

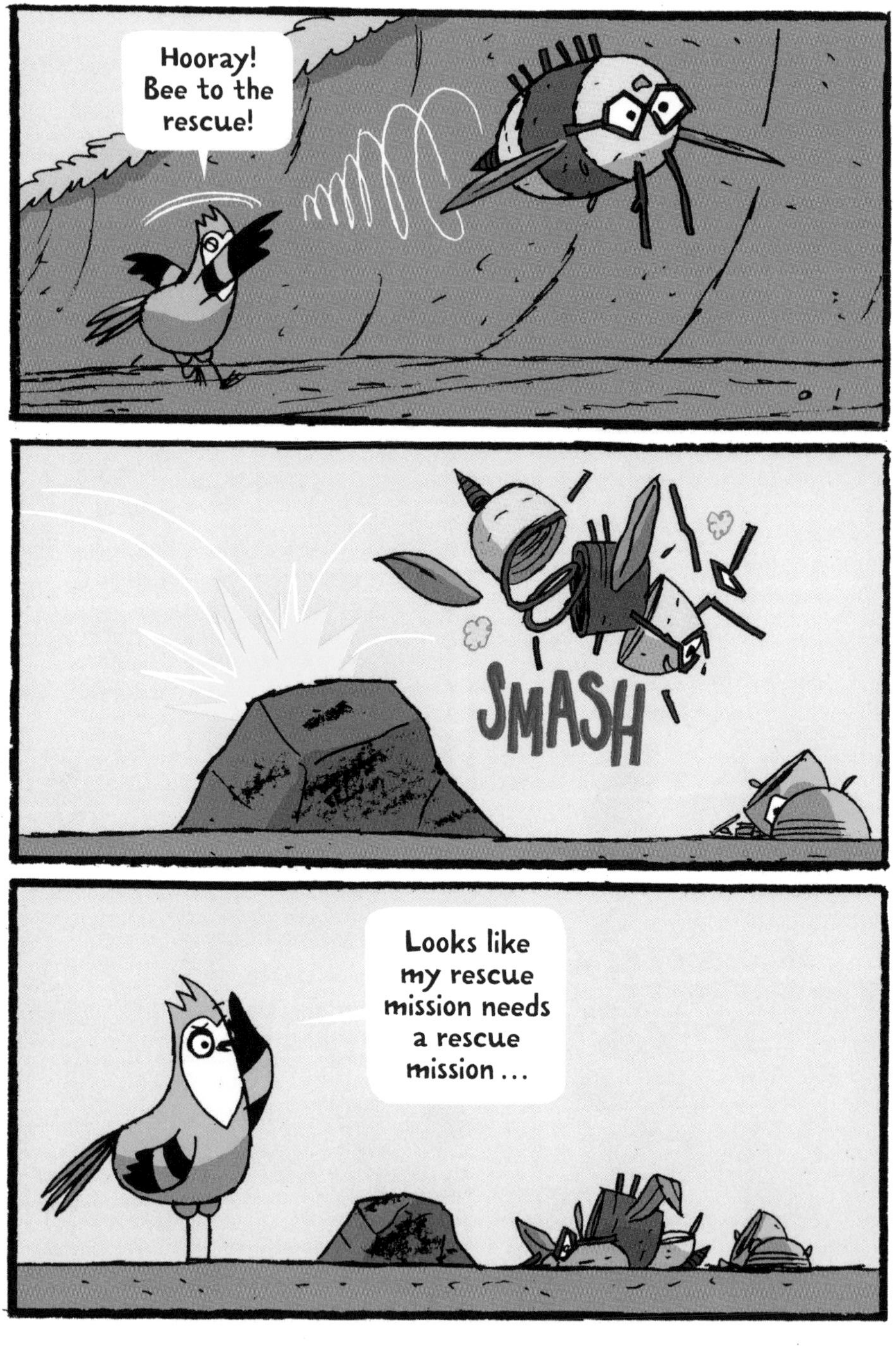
Hooray! Bee to the rescue!
SMASH
Looks like my rescue mission needs a rescue mission . . .

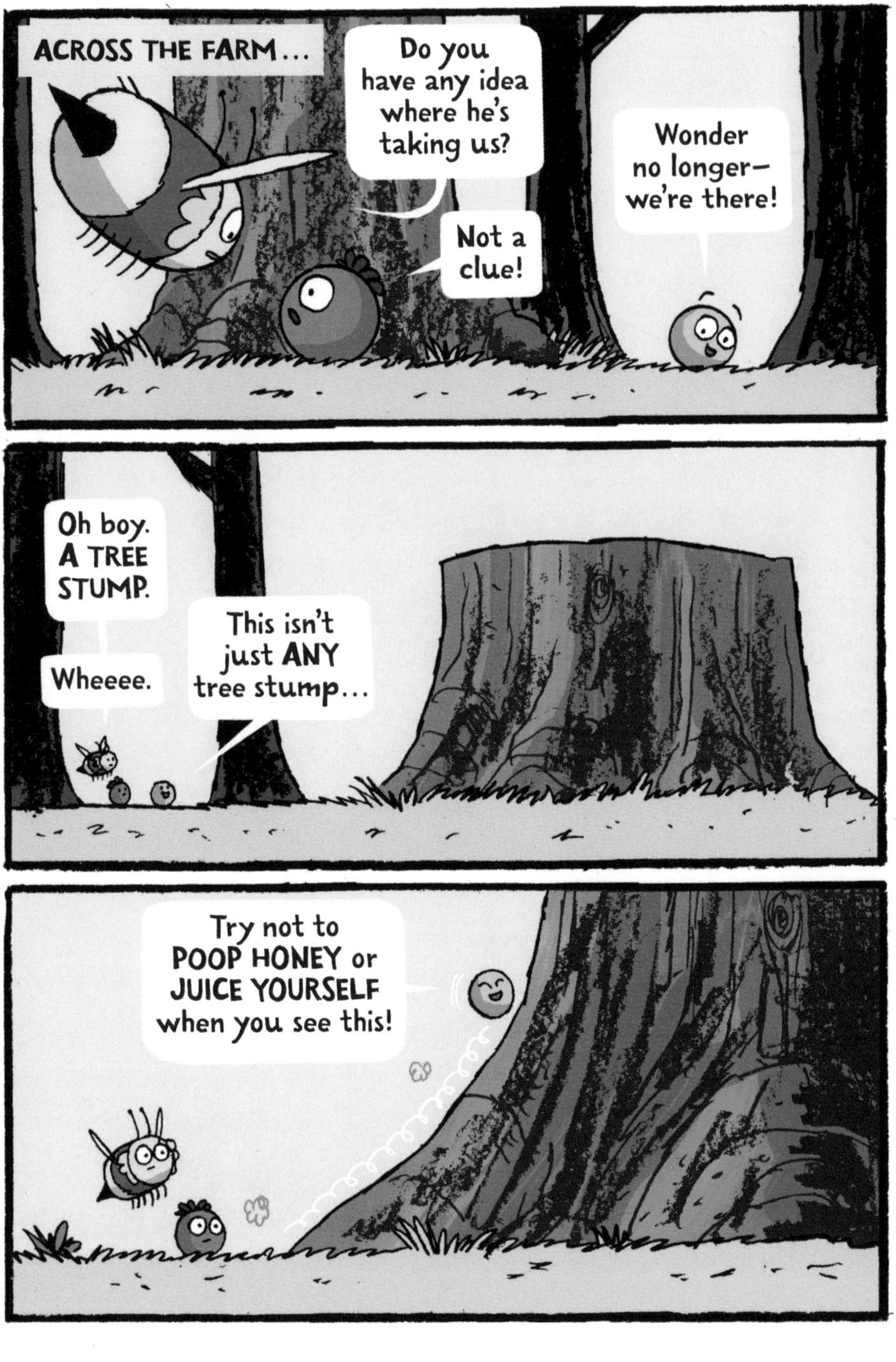
ACROSS THE FARM...
Do you have any idea where he's taking us?
Not a clue!
Wonder no longer—we're there!
Oh boy. A TREE STUMP.
Wheeee.
This isn't just ANY tree stump...
Try not to POOP HONEY or JUICE YOURSELF when you see this!

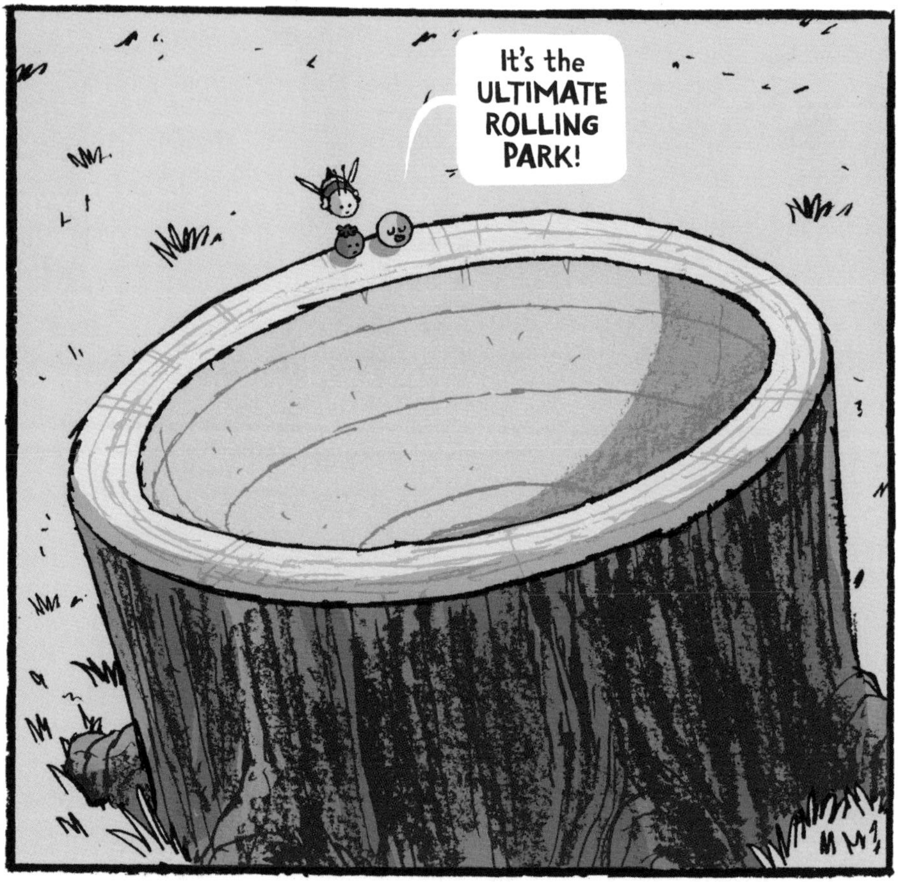
It's the ULTIMATE ROLLING PARK!

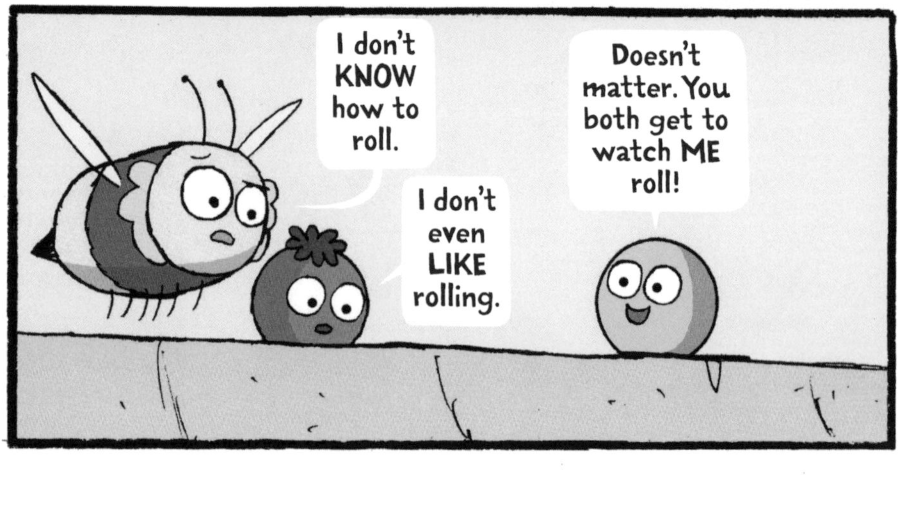
I don't KNOW how to roll.
I don't even LIKE rolling.
Doesn't matter. You both get to watch ME roll!

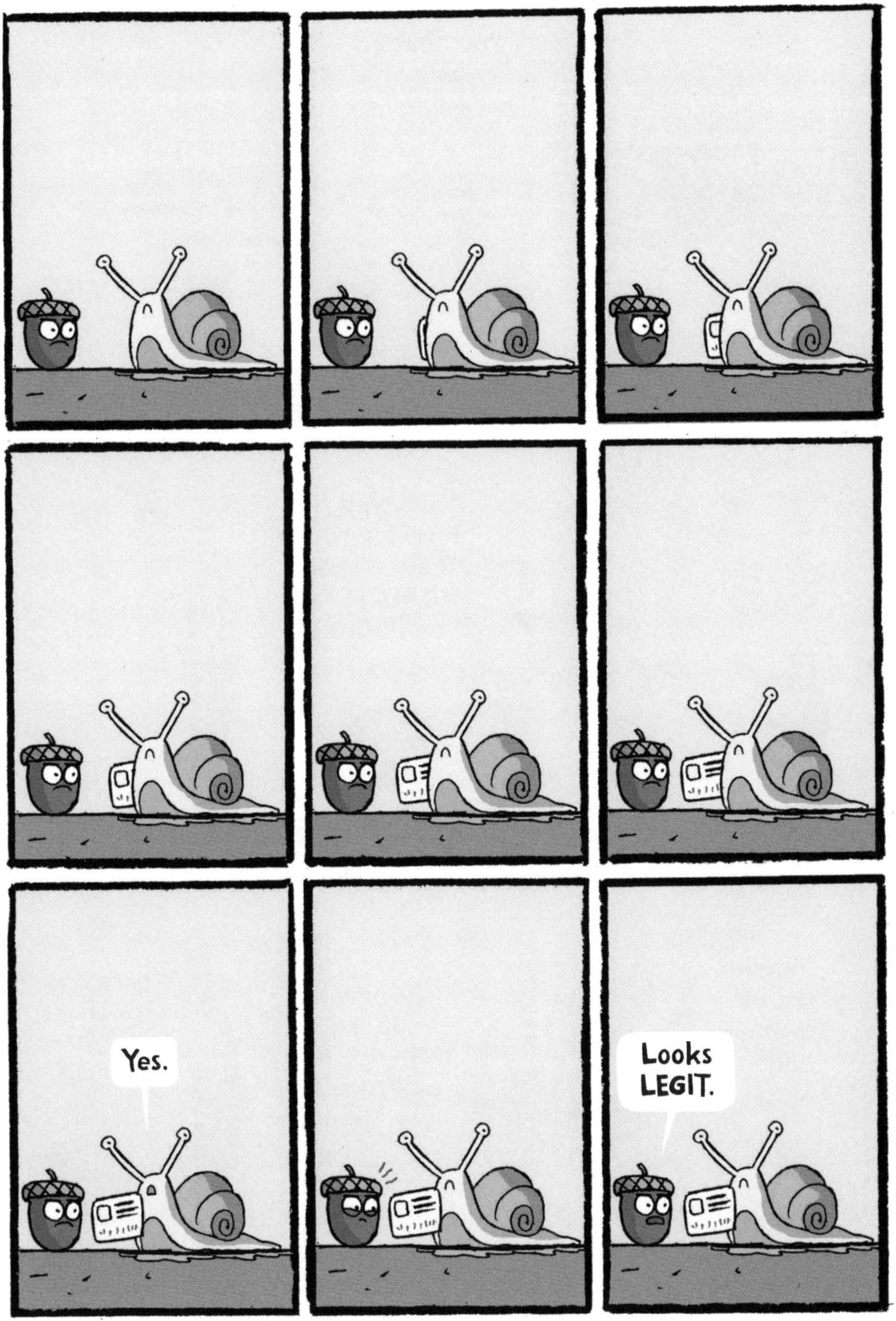
Yes.
Looks LEGIT.

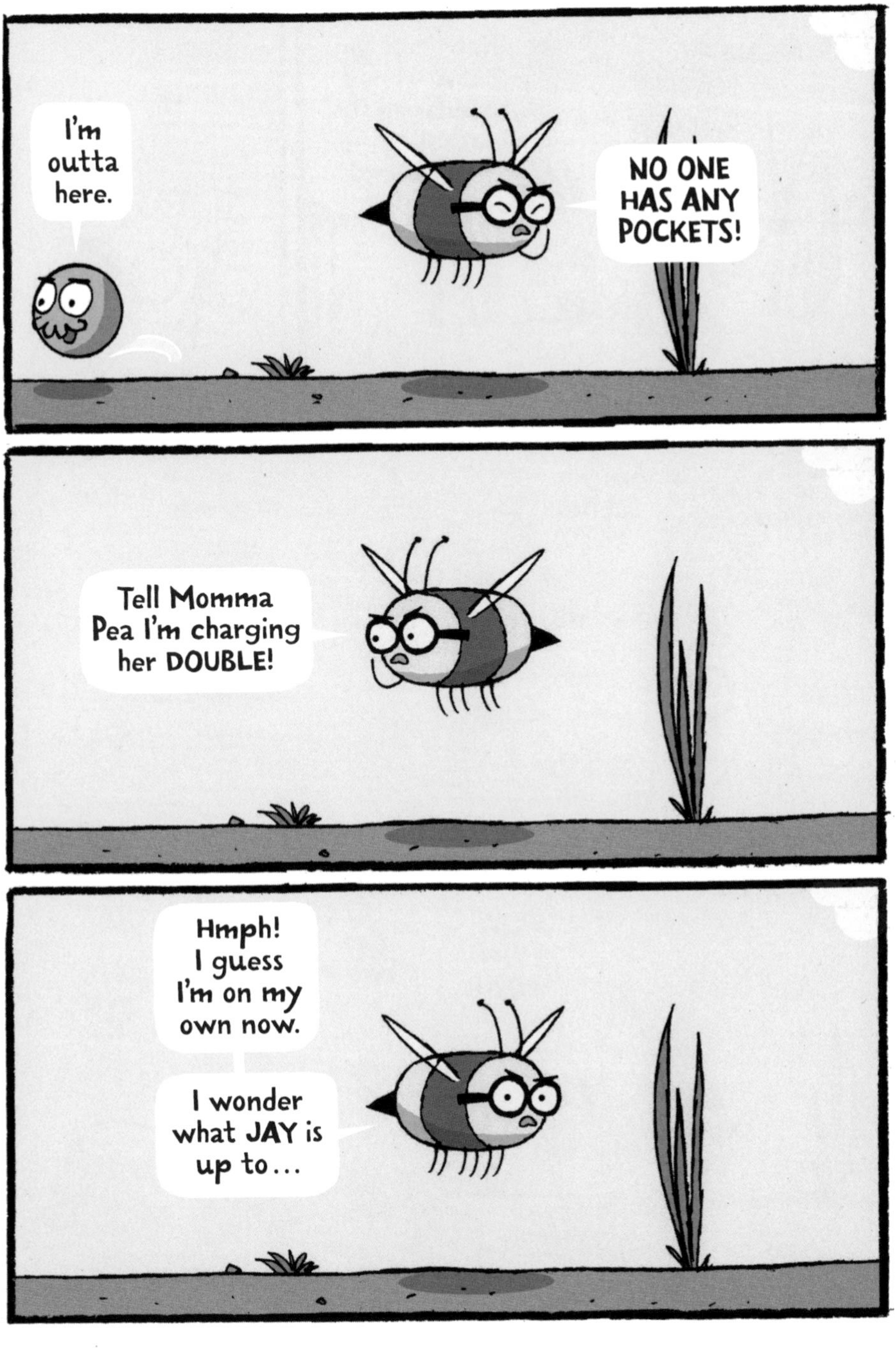
I'm outta here.
NO ONE HAS ANY POCKETS!
Tell Momma Pea I'm charging her DOUBLE!
Hmph! I guess I'm on my own now.
I wonder what JAY is up to...

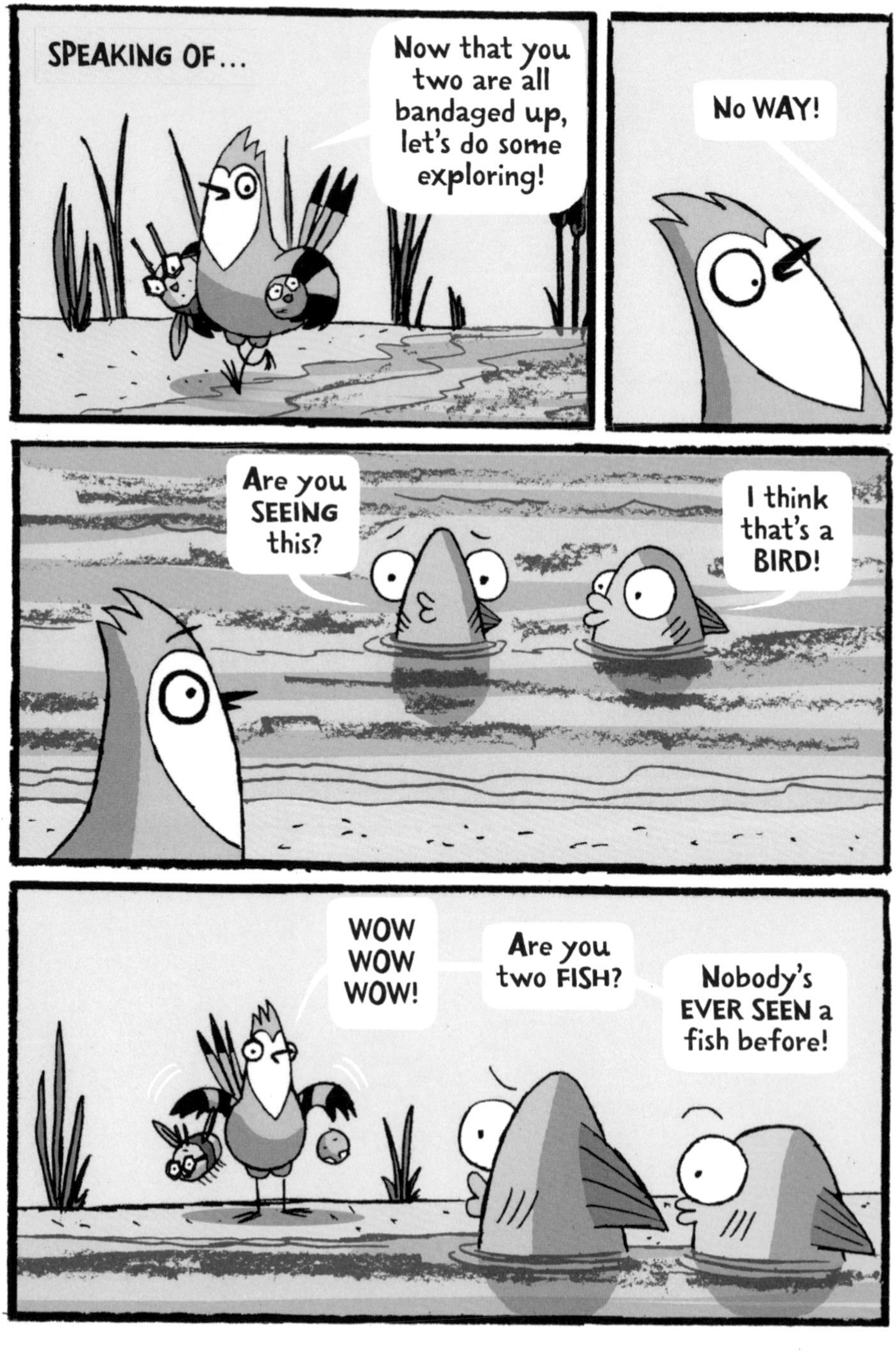
SPEAKING OF...
Now that you two are all bandaged up, let's do some exploring!
No WAY!
Are you SEEING this?
I think that's a BIRD!
WOW WOW WOW!
Are you two FISH?
Nobody's EVER SEEN a fish before!

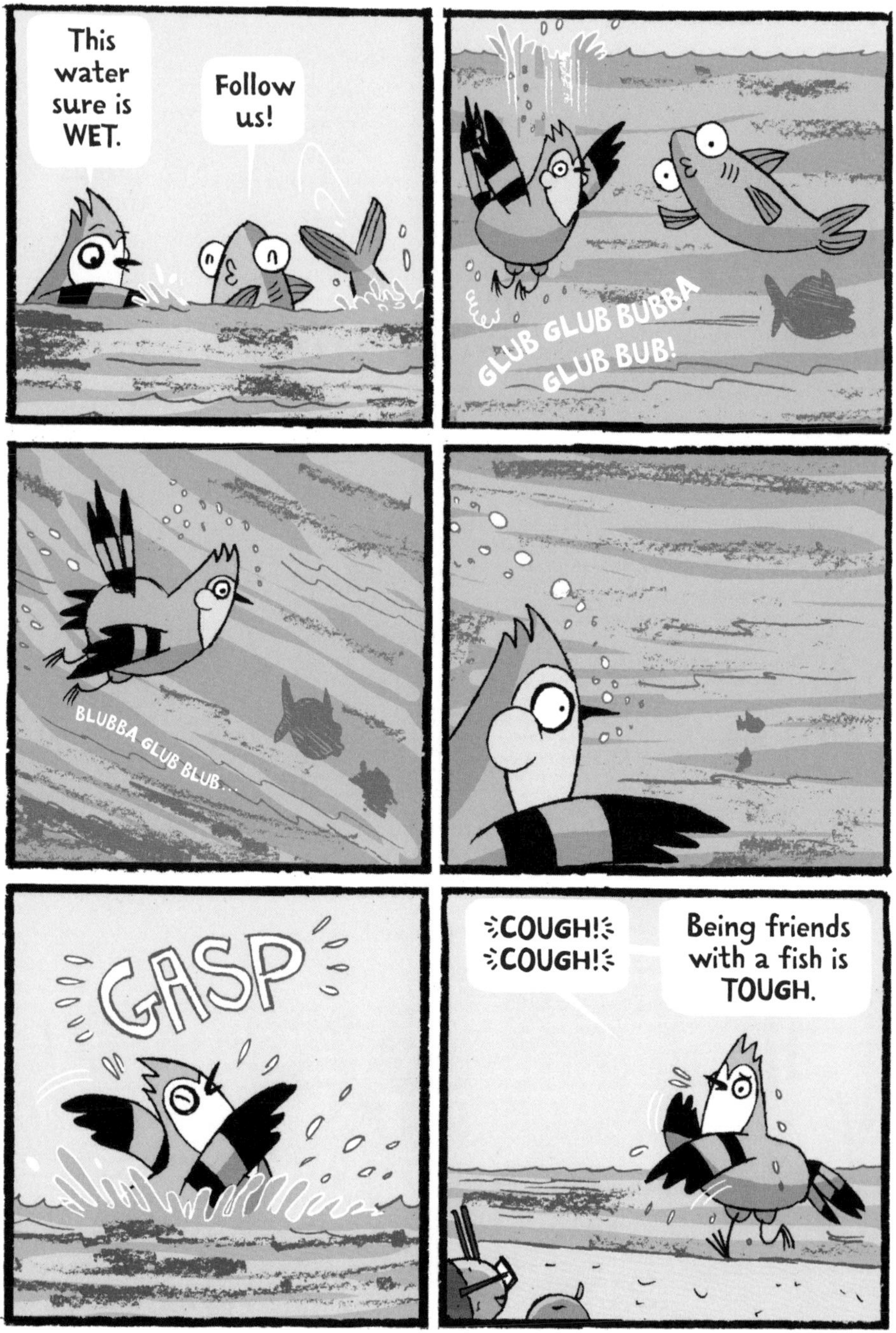
This water sure is WET.
Follow us!
GLUB GLUB BUBBA GLUB BUB!
BLUBBA GLUB BLUB...
GASP
COUGH! COUGH!
Being friends with a fish is TOUGH.

45

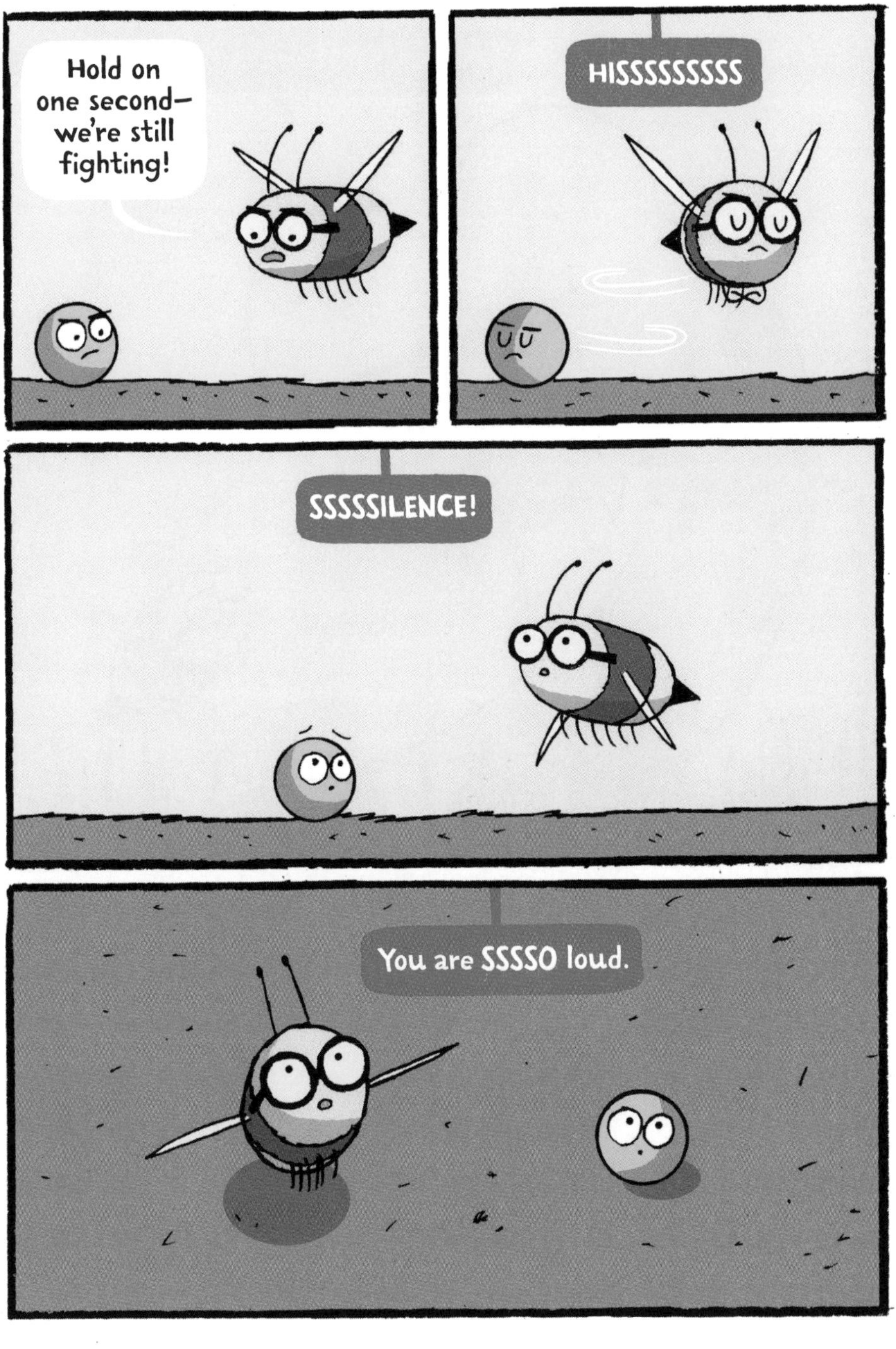
Hold on one second—we're still fighting!
HISSSSSSSSS
SSSSSILENCE!
You are SSSSO loud.

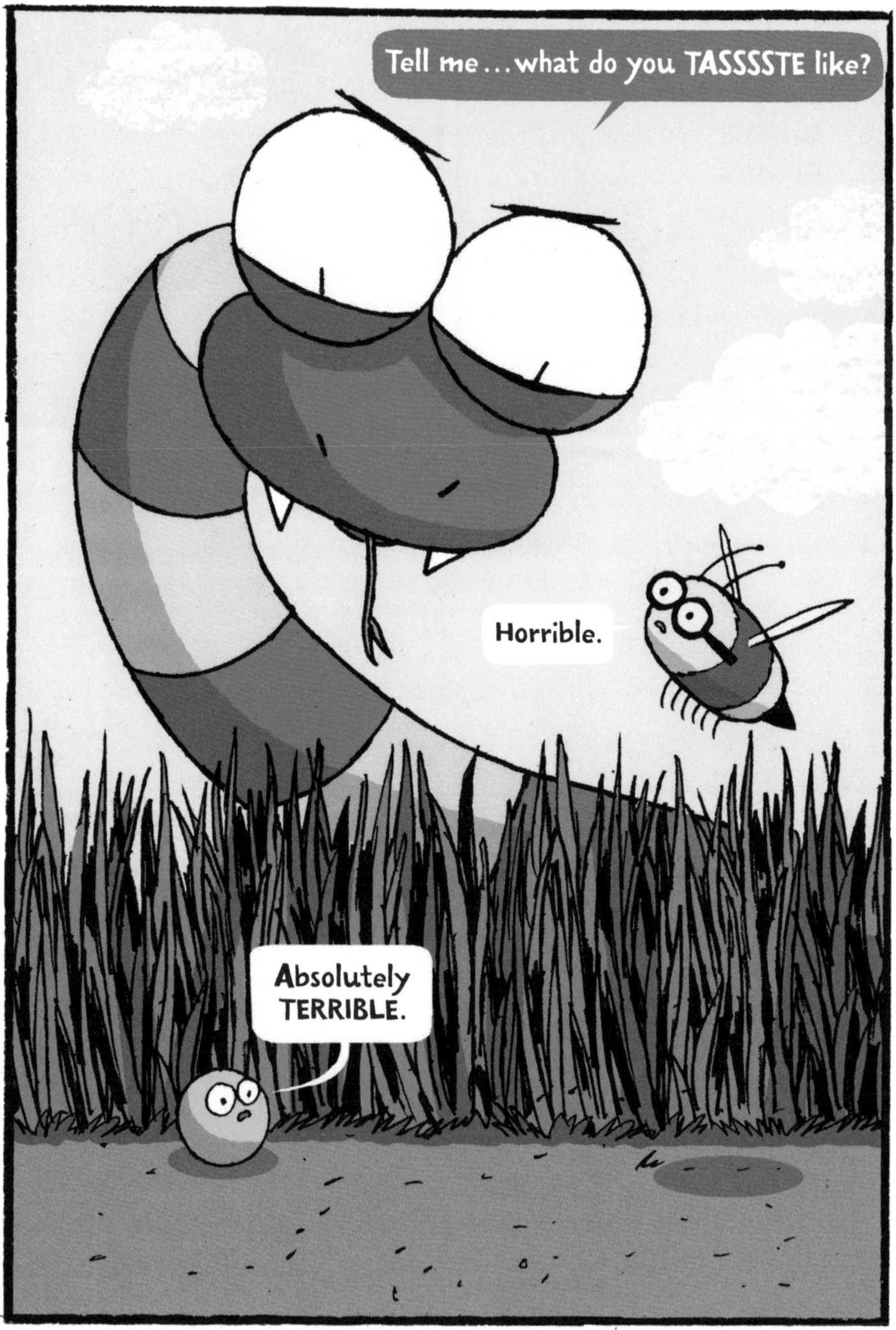
Tell me...what do you TASSSSTE like?
Horrible.
Absolutely TERRIBLE.

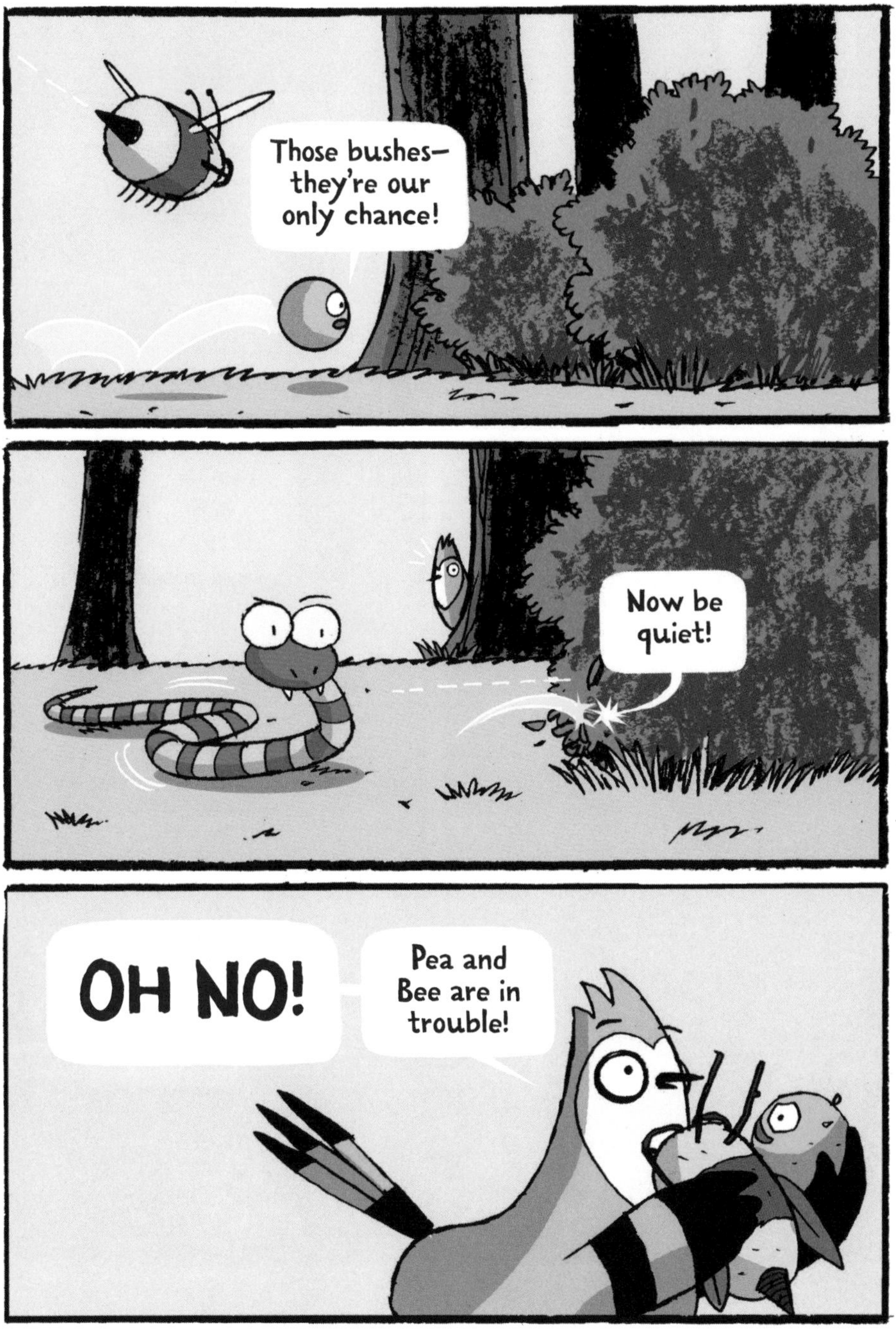
Those bushes—they're our only chance!
Now be quiet!
OH NO!
Pea and Bee are in trouble!

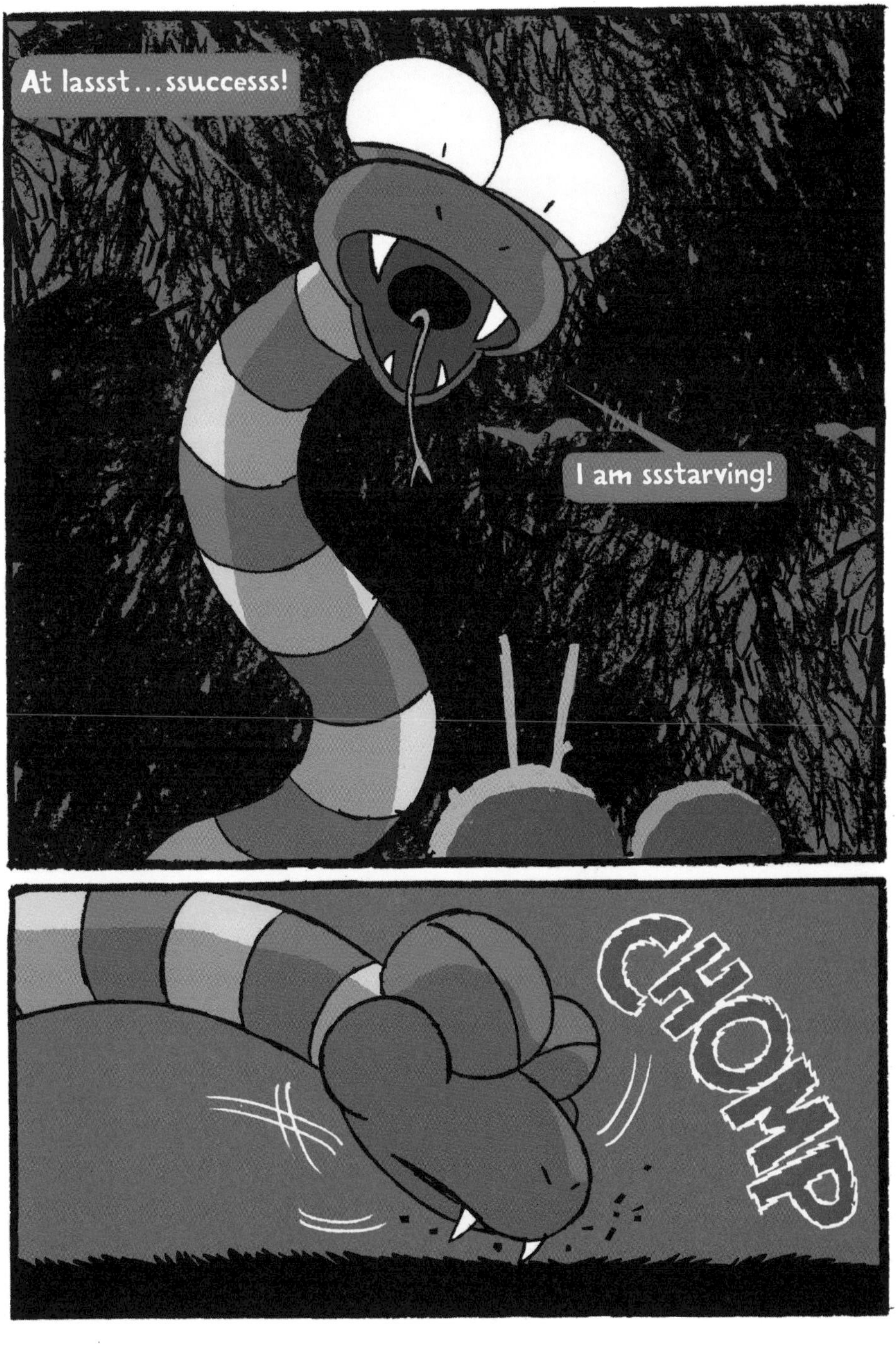
At lassst...ssuccesss!
I am ssstarving!
CHOMP

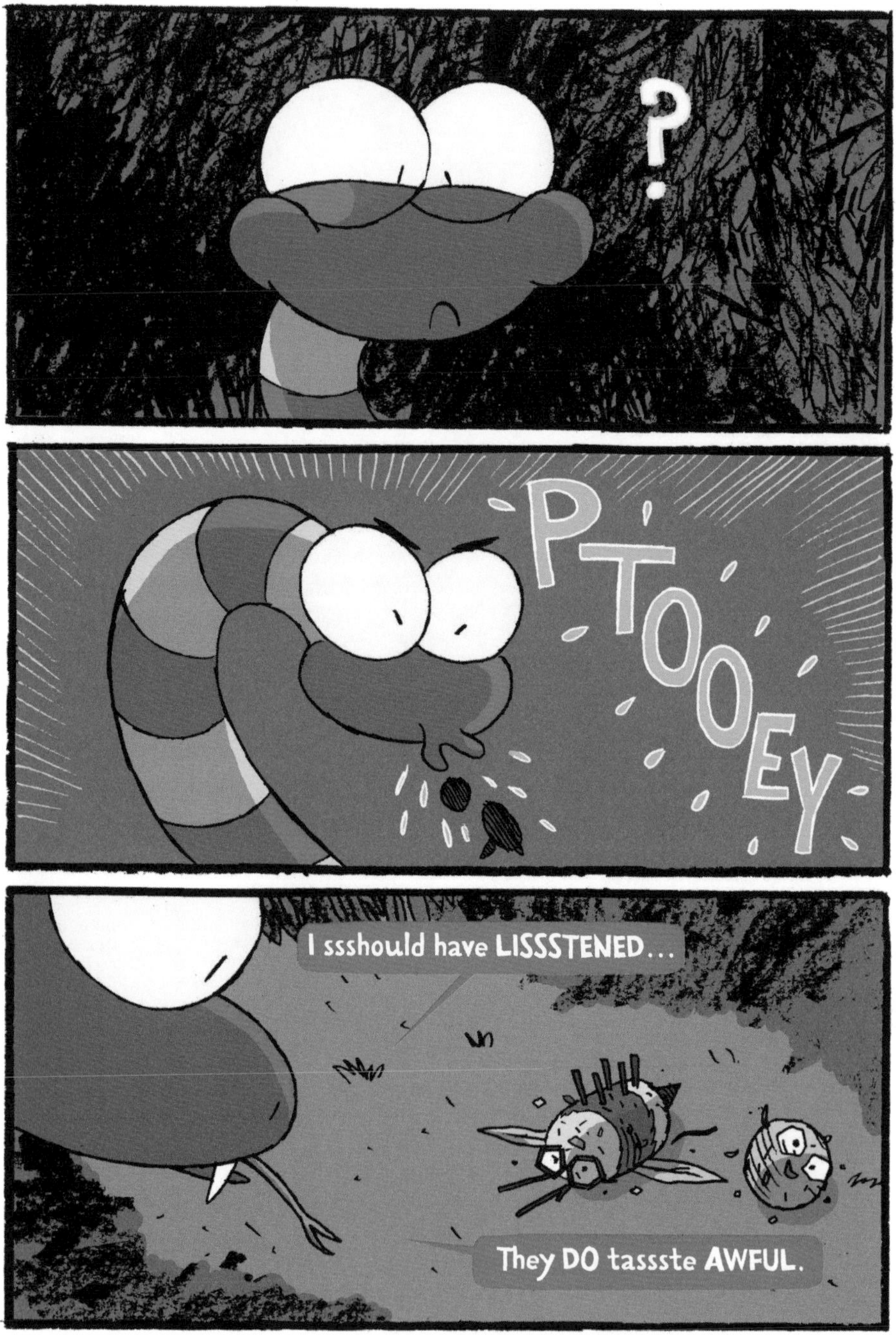
?
PTOOEY
I ssshould have LISSSTENED...
They DO tassste AWFUL.

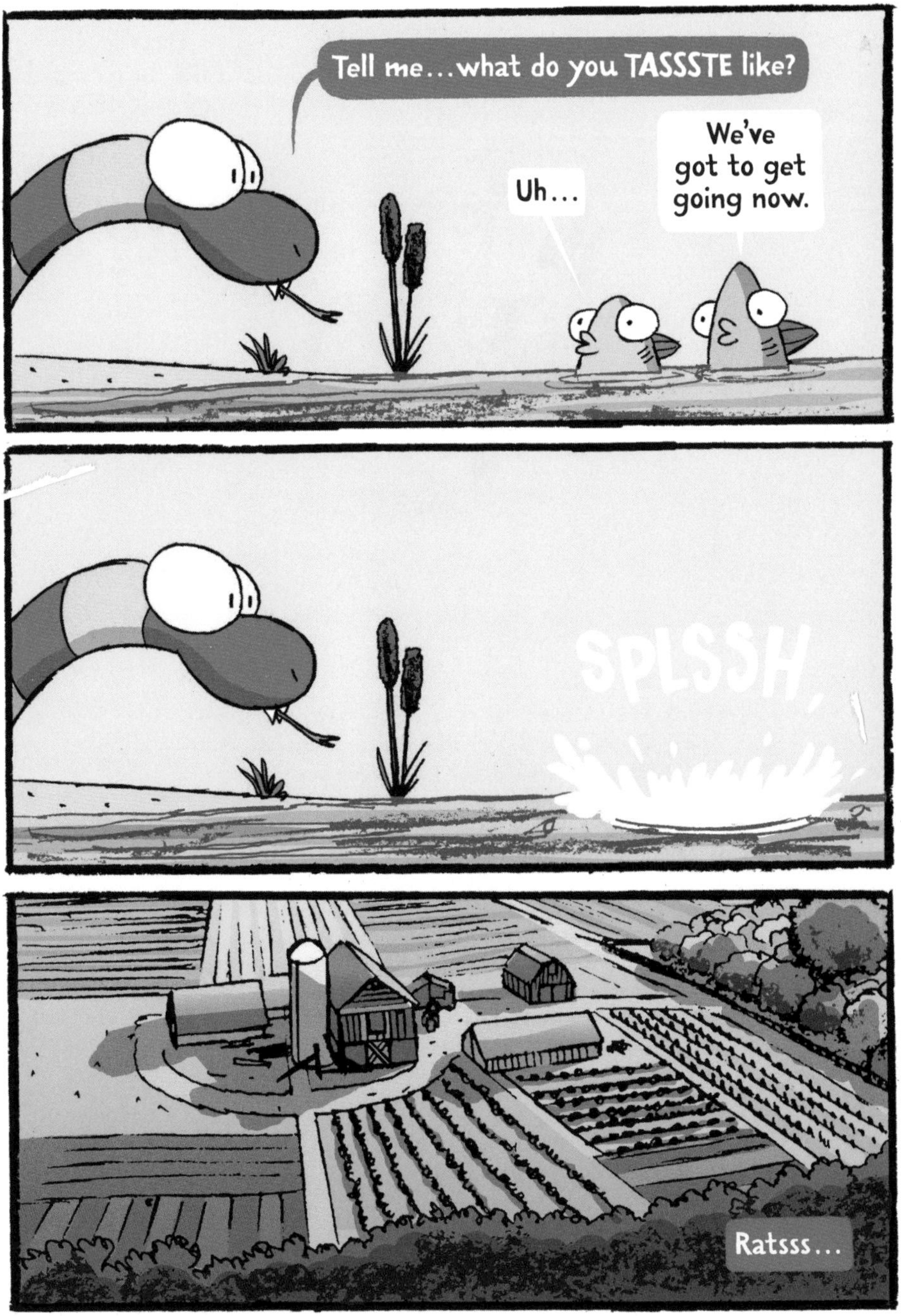
Tell me...what do you TASSSTE like?
Uh...
We've got to get going now.
SPLSSH
Ratsss...

Thank you to Bret Parks, Juliet Parks, Elise Parks,
Robin Parks, and Ssalefish Comics, without whom
this book would not have been possible.

HarperAlley is an imprint of HarperCollins Publishers.

Pea, Bee, & Jay #4: Farm Feud
Copyright © 2022 by Brian Smith
All rights reserved. Printed in Bosnia and Herzegovina.
No part of this book may be used or reproduced in any manner whatsoever without written permission
except in the case of brief quotations embodied in critical articles and reviews. For information address
HarperCollins Children's Books, a division of HarperCollins Publishers, 195 Broadway, New York, NY 10007.
www.harperalley.com

Library of Congress Control Number: 2021941899
ISBN 978-0-06-298126-4 — ISBN 978-0-06-298125-7 (pbk.)

The artist used pencils, paper, a computer, and bee poop (lots and lots
of bee poop) to create the digital illustrations for this book.
Typography by Erica De Chavez
21 22 23 24 25   GPS   10 9 8 7 6 5 4 3 2 1
❖
First Edition